A PERFECT WORLD

Mike North

ISBN 978-1-64559-113-9 (Paperback)
ISBN 978-1-64559-112-2 (Digital)

Copyright © 2019 Mike North
All rights reserved
First Edition

All rights reserved. No part of this publication may be reproduced, distributed, or transmitted in any form or by any means, including photocopying, recording, or other electronic or mechanical methods without the prior written permission of the publisher. For permission requests, solicit the publisher via the address below.

Covenant Books, Inc.
11661 Hwy 707
Murrells Inlet, SC 29576
www.covenantbooks.com

Sam Walker rode his bike as if he was competing in the Tour de France. In his mind, his destination was just as important as winning the yellow jersey. The library had called to say that book number three in The Phantom Narratives series had arrived. Sam was going to be the very first person to check out the newest novel. As he approached the library, he jumped off his bike before it had even come to a complete stop. Sam fumbled with the chain and lock as he hurried to get his bike secured. He knew his mom would not be pleased with him if it were stolen. He also realized that there would be no replacement coming. Forcing himself to take slow, deep breaths, he methodically wound the chain around the bike and attached the lock.

 Entering the library at a controlled pace, he remembered to duck as he passed through the door. It came automatically for him now when he entered a room. At six foot seven, everyone expected him to play basketball, but he would much rather read a good book any day. He moved deliberately slow so no one would be able to see just how excited he really was. He gave an acknowledging nod to the librarian at the desk as he sauntered past rows of romance novels. As soon as she was out of view, he hurried over to the shelf where the reserved books sat. After anxiously searching for the copy with his name on it for a few seconds, he spotted his book. Breathing a sigh of relief, he snatched it up and immediately headed for the self-checkout station by the door. Sam was thankful that those stations had been installed. Now he didn't have to speak to a librarian or reveal his taste in novels. His goal was to get out of the library without being noticed by any more people. He quietly walked out the door, unchained his bike, and headed home. He finally had what he had wanted for so long. If Mom would let him, he hoped to read at least a couple of chapters tonight. Sam pulled his bike around to the garage and entered the house, hoping to get up to his room before he was noticed.

Sam opened the door slowly, hoping that his mom wouldn't hear him come in. If she was occupied with Facebook or texting a friend, he might be able to pull it off. As Sam silently closed the door, he turned and saw his mom standing in the kitchen looking at him; all his hopes of sneaking into his room were suddenly dashed. She had on one of her favorite dresses and had obviously spent time on her hair and makeup. It was then he noticed a man was sitting on the living room couch. "Sam, I want you to come and meet Kenneth," she said excitedly.

Sam walked over to the living room and offered a handshake to Kenneth. "Nice to meet you." Sam had learned long ago to be nice and polite to Mom's new friends. If it made Mom happy, it was worth pretending that he was okay with her dating some loser. This guy would be gone within six months if the pattern held true. Kenneth was a big man with a beer belly hanging out over his belt. It appeared that he hadn't shaved or showered in a few days. A fairly typical choice, all things considered.

"I'm going to fix Kenneth some supper. Did you want me to make some for you too?"

"What are you cooking tonight, Mom?"

"My famous meatloaf," she answered with a proud smile.

Sam never had the heart to tell her just what he thought about the meatloaf. With any luck, this would speed up the breakup of her romance with Kenneth. "No, thanks, Mom. It's tempting, but I'm not very hungry now. I can grab a bite later. I think I will just head to my room now."

"Why don't you keep Kenneth company while I'm in the kitchen?"

The tone of her voice meant that this was not a suggestion. Sam sat down across from Kenneth. An uncomfortable silence filled the room. Sam desperately searched for a conversation starter. "So where did you two meet?"

Kenneth gave Sam a menacing look. "Listen, kid. I don't like wimpy boys that spend their time reading," he said, glancing at Sam's library book. "You should be riding dirt bikes or tearing apart engines. Things that help you live in the real world. Got it?"

"Yes, sir, I think I do. Can I go to my room now?"

"One more thing, kid. I don't want you to mess anything up between your mom and me, or I will rearrange your face."

Sam decided that he liked his face the way it was, so he nodded his head in agreement. "May I be excused?"

"Get out of here already, kid. Stay in your room till after I leave."

"Yes, sir. It was nice meeting you." Sam ran up the stairs, hoping to get to his room before his mom came out of the kitchen.

Sam sat on his bed and opened up his new book. At least Mom would be occupied most of the night, even if it was with someone as annoying as Kenneth. Sam quickly forgot about his troubles as he envisioned himself as one of the characters in The Phantom Narratives, experiencing every adventure that the hero and heroine did.

He had no idea how long he had been reading when his mom's voice brought him back to reality. "Sam, can you come out and talk to me a minute."

"Sure, Mom, what's up?"

"I had a really nice time with Kenneth tonight," she said with a contented smile. "So what did you think of him?"

Sam had known this question was coming, and he pondered how to answer it. "Well, he is a really big guy."

"Yes, he is very strong," she declared with admiration on her face. "Someone who could take care of a woman when she needed it."

"I bet he could rearrange someone's face too," Sam blurted out.

"Honestly, Sam, I don't know where you get these things. I hope your books aren't too violent."

"Sorry, Mom. I don't know where I got that from either."

"I'm really tired," she said with a yawn. "Sleep sounds really good about now. You should probably get to bed soon too. Tomorrow is another school day, you know."

"Don't remind me," Sam groaned. "I want to read a couple more pages before I go to bed."

"Suit yourself, Sam, but I don't want to hear you complaining about how tired you are."

"Would I do that?"

"Yes, you most certainly would, young man." With a wave of her hand, she headed to her bedroom.

Sam opened up his book and started reading again. He told himself that he would read only for fifteen minutes. An hour later, he finally put his novel down. Wouldn't it be awesome to discover a completely new world and escape from this one any time you wanted to? If he could create one, it would be a place of electrifying adventures with opportunities to relax in between. He would have caring, nonjudgmental friends who would support what he wanted to do, not what everyone expected him to do. Maybe in his made up world, he could have two loving parents and a steady girlfriend. Now that would really be a perfect world.

An annoying buzzing next to his bed woke Sam from a sound sleep. Groaning as he struggled to reach the offending alarm without opening his eyes, he was finally able to stop the shrill noise. Relieved, he was tempted to roll over and go back to sleep. Knowing that staying home wasn't an option, he dragged himself out of bed. The fact that it was a Friday took some of the sting out of it. Walking over to his bedroom window, he peered out the blinds. Thankfully, a beautiful sunrise was getting ready to make an appearance. Seeing the cloudless sky brightened his mood. There were benefits in living close to Riverton High. It enabled Sam to ride his bike to school in nice weather. Missing the social interaction of the bus ride was a huge blessing. Being a freshman was not a good thing to be in a group of high school kids within close proximity of each other. At Sam's height, it was impossible to not be noticed, which was what he preferred. His weight or lack of it made him seem even taller. After locking up his bike, he hustled in the door toward his locker.

Walking quickly with his head down to avoid eye contact with anyone, he was jolted out of his path by a large body that slammed him into the lockers next to him. Sam crumpled to the floor as pain erupted all over his body. His books scattered as he tried to clear his vision.

"You should really watch where you're going. You could get hurt next time." Laughter filled the hall as the big guy's friends looked on in amusement. A large hand reached out and grabbed Sam's library book, which Sam had intended to read during study hall. "Well, what have we here? The Phantom Narratives? Isn't that cute. I bet all the kindergartners are jealous of you."

"At least he knows how to read, Josh." A red-haired girl stood in front of Sam as he got up off the floor. With anger burning in her eyes, she grabbed the book out of Josh's hand in one quick motion. "Picking on people doesn't make you a big man. It just proves how weak you really are."

Just as Josh was starting to respond, one of the teachers came down the hallway to see what the commotion was. Josh glared at the red-headed girl. He and his buddies headed toward the gym while Sam gathered his belongings.

"Thanks," he said to the girl, but she had already disappeared into a nearby classroom. He gathered everything and glanced at the clock. With a big sigh, he resigned himself to the fact that he was already late.

Sneaking silently into his math class, he found an empty chair near the back. Because of his height, no one wanted him sitting in front of them. Just when he thought that he had successfully escaped detection, a deep voice called out his name. "Glad you could join us, Mr. Walker."

Every head turned to get a glimpse of Sam's reaction. He wished he could somehow disappear from view. Embarrassment registered on his face as he offered up an apology to Mr. Cummings, who seemed to take great pleasure from Sam's discomfort. Finally, Mr. Cummings left him alone and returned to today's lesson. The rest of the class lost interest in seeing Sam squirm, so he was able to concentrate on what was being taught. Math had never been on his list of favorite classes, and now because of Mr. Cummings, it ranked lower still.

Of all his classes, English was by far the most interesting to him. The fact that Miss Collins, who had just joined the teaching ranks fresh out of school, was his teacher, made it even more enjoyable. Of any of his instructors, he liked her the most. Being closer in age to her students made her more relatable to them. The thing that Sam appreciated the most was that she obviously cared about each person, regardless of their social standing. Best of all, she encouraged him to dream about the possibilities instead of dwelling on what couldn't be accomplished. Someday, he would become a success at something and make a good life for himself. Whatever that might look like.

When he arrived home, his mom had already left for work, which was fine with Sam. He didn't want to have another confrontation today. As he searched for an after school snack, he found his mind wandering back to the girl who had stood up for him. She probably stood about a foot shorter than Josh and definitely was many pounds lighter than him, but she was not intimidated at all. While he admired her courage, it caused him to feel ashamed that he hadn't stuck up for himself. Maybe he wasn't quite ready yet to take on the world like the Phantom did in his adventures.

For many kids his age, Friday night was a night to party or hang out with friends. Sam, however, anticipated being alone and doing whatever he felt like at the moment as long as that didn't involve money or a vehicle to ride in. Reluctantly, Sam went over to the bulletin board in the kitchen. Almost every Friday, Mom's Saturday chore list hung on it like a dark cloud directly over his head, threatening to rain on his day. Since they could not afford to hire anyone to do any of the tasks, the burden fell on Sam. Many of the projects involved their run-down house, even when he had no qualifications or experience to complete the job correctly. Trudging over to gaze at the list, he let out a groan when he saw the staggering amount of things that his mom had come up with for this weekend. Reluctantly, he decided to go to bed soon so he could get an early start. Anger descended on him as he crawled into bed. It was extremely tiring trying to survive every day when it seemed everyone else was enjoying the moment. Exhaustion eventually took over as Sam fell asleep.

Saturday morning came too soon for Sam. He dragged himself out of bed early so he could get started on Mom's list. He figured that if he got going right away, he might have some time to himself later. He went downstairs and saw the list sitting on the counter waiting for him. With a sinking feeling in his stomach, he slowly reached out and took a look at what was facing him today. When he saw how many projects were on it, he felt anger surge through his body. He wanted to throw something, but he restrained himself. Dad should be doing these chores not him. Why did Dad have to leave? Sam wasn't sure who he should be more upset with, his mom or his dad. With a sigh, he headed outside to start on his outdoor work before it got too warm.

Sam had just finished mowing when his mom came out of the house with a water bottle. "How's it going?"

"I just finished number four on the list. Only eight more to go," he said in a slightly sarcastic tone.

"Sam, have I told you how proud of you I am? You have had to be the man of the house way before you should have been." With tears in her eyes, she gave Sam a hug. "I am truly sorry."

"I know, Mom. It's just the way things are right now."

"There's leftover meatloaf in the fridge if you get hungry. I'm going to get groceries now. You remember it's my turn to work at the bar tonight, right?"

He nodded his head. "I wish you didn't work there."

"Me too, Sam," she said with a sad expression. "It's not the way things were supposed to turn out." She headed back into the house as Sam took a swig from the water bottle. Bitterness rose up inside him as she disappeared. It definitely shouldn't have turned out this way.

After Sam had completed all his tasks, he plopped down on the couch, exhausted by the seemingly endless amount of work he had accomplished. As hunger enveloped him, he decided to pass on the meatloaf once again and order a pizza instead. Mom paid him a small amount for helping out around the house, so he had enough money to get the pizza delivered. Besides, as he was only a freshman, he was too young to drive. Not that he could afford a car anyway.

As he waited for the pizza, he pulled out his book and began to read. Instantly, he lost himself in his novel. The hero was a young man that had become a secret agent for the United States government. When a lone operative was needed to work on a covert operation, the Phantom was there to save the day. The forces of evil knew of his existence, but he would disappear before he could be captured or have his identity revealed. Sam sighed. If only he could have a little bit of excitement in his life.

On Sunday morning, Sam woke up to his alarm and hopped in the shower. He wanted to be ready when his Uncle Jason came to pick him up for church. Uncle Jason was his mom's brother. In some ways, he had become a surrogate dad to him. Because Uncle Jason traveled a lot with his job, Sam didn't see him near as much as he wanted to. When he was in town, he made sure to take Sam with him to church. After Sam got out of the shower, he noticed his mom's room was still dark. He shook his head in frustration.

"Mom, it's time to get up and get ready for church." When he did not get a response, he went to her door and pounded on it.

"Sam, please let me sleep," she groaned in a weak voice.

"But you will miss church again," he protested.

"I had a long night at work, and I just need to rest and recover from it," she pleaded. "You go without me this time."

"I go without you almost every time," he said in an angry tone.

"Please, just go without me. I promise I will go next week."

"Sure, Mom, whatever," he muttered under his breath. "Next week."

Sam heard the sound of Uncle Jason's wheels bouncing over the crumbling driveway as he pulled up to the house. He went out to meet him, and before his uncle had a chance to turn off the car, he opened the front passenger door and hopped in.

"Wow, you're in a hurry! Is there a famous guest speaker that I wasn't told about preaching today? Or maybe you have found the woman of your dreams, and you're in a rush to see her again." Uncle Jason grinned at Sam, looking for a response to his teasing.

"I just need to get out of that house for a while."

"It doesn't have anything to do with your mom, does it?"

Sam sighed as he explained that his mom slept in again. "Sometimes, I feel like she's the child, and I'm the adult," he complained. "I worry about her wasting her life with all these people she meets at the bar."

With an understanding look in his eyes, Uncle Jason replied, "To be honest, Sam, so do I."

When Sam returned from church, the house was quiet. He looked around to see where his mom was, but there was no sign of her anywhere. Puzzled by her absence, he decided to check the garage. Her car was gone. He went back inside to look for a note. After searching for a while, he saw a piece of paper on the floor. It must have fallen when she shut the door to the garage. She had to have been in quite a hurry for it to end up there. Sam picked up the note and read it. She had gone to see Kenneth. He crumpled it up and hurled it in the direction of the trash can. Amazing how quickly her attitude about getting out of bed had changed. With resignation, he headed to the refrigerator to fix himself lunch.

His mood brightened when he realized he would have lots of time to read his book. Maybe he would even finish it today. After reading for quite a while, he made himself supper. His mom had still not returned from her date with Kenneth. He decided to read a little more while he waited for her to come home. Sam began to get drowsy, but knowing that he wouldn't sleep well until he was sure she was safe, he laid on their beat-up old couch. Finally, she came through the door. Surprised to see him up, she started to give her excuse. Not wanting a disagreement this late at night, Sam gave his mom a wave and silently went to his room. Maybe they could discuss it tomorrow.

Sam awoke to bright light shining in his face. He reached for the covers to shield himself, but they weren't there. Forcing himself to open his eyes, he glanced at his surroundings. He was lying outdoors in tall grass. Startled, he quickly jumped to his feet. To his left was a field full of flowers. Many different variations dotted the landscape. Multiple shades of roses, brightly colored daffodils, and extremely large sunflowers were some of the species that caught Sam's eye. Uniquely shaped versions of familiar favorites in colors he couldn't even begin to describe shone brilliantly. Shades of reds, yellows, and oranges mixed with more exotic colors such as lavender, turquoise, and even silver to dazzle the eyes. The display went on as far as Sam could see. To his right, a dense forest covered the landscape, with every type of tree seemingly represented. Some of the trees were gigantic, at least as tall as any redwood could be. Trees that would only grow in fertile soil stood next to gnarled bristlecone pines and other species that preferred sandy soil. Red buds, oaks, and maples stood beside tulip trees and catalpas with their massive leaves. Sequoias dwarfed bright-red Japanese maples growing nearby with their enormous width.

Turning around, Sam stood frozen at the sight of snowcapped mountains towering majestically into the sky. Waterfalls could be seen cascading down the jagged rock outcroppings. The entire mountain shone with a translucent glow that lit up the surrounding area. After tearing himself away from the beautiful mountain view, Sam discovered a scenic, rolling meadow with a large area full of green grass that appeared to have been freshly mowed. The grass was so perfectly trimmed that it almost looked artificial to Sam. He suddenly realized that he was no longer in his pajamas but instead, was fully clothed in the shirt and pants he had been preparing to wear to school. He felt so confused by what was happening that he had no idea what to do next.

A voice behind him made him jump. "Let's go, it's time for the game. We don't want to be late." Sam turned around to see a short Hispanic boy about his age standing next to him. Seeing Sam's puzzled expression, the boy stuck out his hand. "You must be new here. I'm Juan. What's your name?"

"Sam," he said, still trying to take in everything. "Where are we, and how did I get here?"

Juan laughed. "No time for questions now. Come on, let's head to the field."

Juan took off running toward the inviting green grass. Not wanting to be left on his own, Sam ran as fast as he could to try to catch Juan. As he got close to the field, he could see other kids arriving, every conceivable size, shape, and ethnic background imaginable represented there. Everyone was laughing and talking at once. By the time Sam got to the field, he was out of breath. He plopped down on the ground in exhaustion. As he scanned the area, he noticed that one of the boys had brought a soccer ball with him. Evidently, there soon would be a soccer match. It was then he saw the nets on each side of the field.

Sam walked up to Juan, who was talking to a tall, thin black boy and a girl of Japanese descent. "Here is our new friend, Sam." Juan pointed to the tall boy. "This is Bakari, and over there is Hatsuko."

Bakari smiled broadly. "Welcome, friend. We are very happy that you will be playing with us."

Hatsuko bowed and gave him a little wave. "Very pleased to meet you," she said in a shy voice.

After acknowledging the greetings, Sam pulled Juan aside. "Maybe I will just watch everyone play. I am not very good."

Juan laughed. "That does not matter here. We don't care how good you play." Juan gave him an encouraging smile. "You can be on our team this time."

Not wanting to disappoint Juan, Sam reluctantly agreed. As if summoned by an invisible buzzer, everyone started to take a spot on the field. All of them seemed to know what team they were on and what position they would play. There was no arguing or discussion of any kind. Sam filled the last available spot on Juan's team, the left forward position. Next to him, at center, was an athletic-looking girl with long blond hair tied up in a ponytail. Sam tried to take deep breaths to calm his nerves. The game was about to begin.

Sam had no delusions of scoring goals or even making a great play. His goal was to survive without embarrassing himself. The blond girl next to him was unbelievably talented. The ball seemed to stick to her feet like it was tied with a string. Bakari was the forward on the opposite side of the blond. As she made a rush down the field, she drew the defense toward her and then made a perfect pass to Bakari. He instantly sent the ball across the field to Sam who had no one near him. Here was his chance! He took a few dribbles and decided to shoot before the defense caught up with him. With a swift kick, he connected with the ball. It dribbled off his foot about two feet in front of him. His momentum took him to the ball's path, and he tripped and fell. His face beet red, he expected laughter or disapproving comments from his teammates. While the ball headed down the other direction, the goalie of the opposing team came over to where he lay.

"Are you all right?" he said with a concerned look on his face. He extended his hand and helped Sam up.

"Except for my pride, I guess."

"Don't worry about it. You can't score every time." Sam ran back toward midfield, hoping for an opportunity to redeem himself.

The game continued for at least an hour when, without warning, everyone stopped playing and headed off the field. Sam sent Juan a puzzled glance. Juan answered his unspoken question. "Halftime break, my friend. Come, follow us," he said with a wave of his hand.

Sam watched as both teams walked toward a grove of trees behind the south side of the field. He walked over slowly, unsure of where everyone was going. He heard Juan and some of his teammates call out his name as they motioned for him to follow. Sam found a small path that everyone was using to navigate their way through the thick group of trees. He came to a clearing where a beautiful small lake glistened in the sunlight. Marveling at how crystal clear the water was, he ventured over to the lake's edge. Many of the players were drinking from it and splashing some on themselves. He debated whether or not he should join them.

"Go ahead and take a drink. Don't be afraid. The water is pure and safe."

Walking up to him was the athletic blond girl that he had been playing next to. "Have you ever seen a more lovely lake than this one?" she asked. The blond girl moved closer. "Good job getting open for that shot," she commented in an encouraging tone. "I'm Chelsea," she said as she took a seat on the ground. "Juan tells me you're new here."

Sam nodded as he got down on his knees, cupped the water in his hands, and began to drink. After he had quenched his thirst, Sam found a spot next to Chelsea. Gazing at the beautiful scenery, Sam turned to Chelsea with a confused expression on his face. "Where are we?"

She smiled and shrugged her shoulders. "Don't try to figure it out. Just enjoy it."

While he was pondering his next question, he heard a faint voice off in the distance calling his name. He glanced around him, but he saw no one. Suddenly, the voice got louder, and his vision began to blur. "Sam, wake up! You're going to be late for school!"

He opened his eyes and tried to focus. His mom was in his room, trying to wake him up. "Wow, you were in such a deep sleep, you didn't even hear your alarm going off."

Sam glanced at the clock and then leaped out of bed in a panic. "I guess I was really tired," he said as he scrambled to get everything together. Sam shook his head in disbelief. His dream had seemed so real. Why couldn't he have stayed there?

After eating breakfast, Sam pulled out his bike for the ride to school. As he pulled up to the bike stand outside the front of the building, he vowed not to be an easy target this time. Walking carefully through the hall, he kept his head held high and tried to be aware of his surroundings at all times. On his way to science class, he saw the red-headed girl that came to his defense. He was going to call out her name until he realized he had no idea what it was. He hurried over and caught up to her before she could get in to her classroom. He reached out and touched her arm, causing her to turn around.

"I just wanted to thank you for helping me yesterday," he stammered.

"No problem. I just can't stand bullies or people that think they are better than anyone else. It makes me so mad, I tend to get a little carried away sometimes. Besides, I like to read too," she said with a mischievous grin. "Bye, Sam. We'll see you around."

As she started to walk away, Sam realized he didn't even know what to call her. As if she had read his mind, she turned and said, "I'm Valerie."

Sam went and sat down in class. It hit him all at once. Valerie actually knew who he was, at least well enough to call him by name. Maybe she even liked him a little bit. He smiled to himself as he tried to focus on his teacher. It wasn't going to be easy.

When Sam arrived home, his mom was getting ready for work. Her hours and the days she worked varied, but it was always an evening shift. That was when the bars were filled with people unwinding from their own jobs or hanging out with friends. It was also the time that men went out to search for some female companionship. Because his mom was a waitress in a predominantly male atmosphere, she never had a problem attracting interest from one of the customers. Unfortunately, most were not very good candidates for a stable, long-term relationship. Sam continually worried about her safety and hoped that she wouldn't bring anyone home. His attempts to get her to quit failed miserably. Every time he brought up the subject, she would end the conversation by claiming that she couldn't do anything else. He suspected her real reason for working there was to find another husband.

Sam noticed that she was taking extra time tonight. He figured she probably was trying to impress someone. His suspicions were confirmed when he saw her preening in front of the full-length mirror in her room. She stopped when she saw him watching her. "You scared me. I didn't hear you come in."

"It's probably because you were singing to yourself," he said with a smirk on his face. Unable to keep the sarcasm out of his voice, he asked her if she had a date after work.

"I may be a little later tonight. Ken promised to be there to see me."

"Who is Ken?"

"You should know. You met him a few nights ago."

"I thought his name was Kenneth. When did you start calling him Ken?"

"Don't get smart with me, young man." Her face softened. "I know you worry about me, but I'm a big girl."

"He is a pretty big guy too."

"I'm done discussing this," she said with a weary voice. "You need to do your homework and go to bed early tonight. "I won't be up in time to wake you tomorrow, so don't stay up and wait for me." She waited for an argument but Sam just nodded his head in resignation.

As she got ready to leave, he called out to her. "Please be careful, Mom."

"No need to worry," she reassured him.

When the garage door closed, he softly answered, "You know I will."

After scraping together something to eat, Sam cleaned up his dishes and started with his homework. Trying hard not to rush through everything, he succeeded in getting done early enough to return his book to the library and have some time to search for more reading material. After finding a few promising books by authors that he had not read before, he headed home. Maybe he would start on one of them yet tonight. Bounding up the stairs, Sam enthusiastically laid out his selections in an attempt to decide which one to read first. After much debate, he resorted to randomly picking one with his eyes closed. Opening it up, he began to read. Concentrating proved nearly impossible as his mind wandered back to the previous night. Despite his best efforts, he kept replaying last night's dream in his mind. He could not remember a dream as vivid or long lasting as this one. Strangely enough, he could recall every detail even though, normally, the memories were spotty at best. It never occurred to him that it was only the beginning of his nightly excursions.

A cool breeze gently blew against Sam's face. Shivering, he struggled to wake up enough to go close his bedroom window. Funny, he didn't even remember opening it last night. He had been so tired, he hadn't bothered to change out of his clothes. The sound of birds singing happily and children's voices playing somewhere in the distance jolted him awake. Once again, he was not in his bedroom anymore. He found himself sleeping in some tall grass with a large rock as his pillow. He jumped to his feet when he heard the sound of familiar voices, recognizing Juan and some other kids about his age talking excitedly. As they got closer, he noticed Bakari, Chelsea, and an Arabic girl that he didn't recognize. They were laughing and singing a song in a language Sam did not understand.

"Come on, Sam. We're going mountain climbing today," Juan said in an enthusiastic tone.

Sam hesitated as he pondered his options. Chelsea noticed his indecision. "Have you gotten a better offer today?" she said with a twinkle in her eye.

Realizing that he had no idea what else he would do or where he would go, he quickly agreed to join them. Besides, he enjoyed everyone's company, especially Chelsea's.

"Let's race to the mountain!" hollered Juan as he took off down a narrow tree-lined path. Everyone else instantly joined in, including Sam.

The others had arrived at the base of the mountain by the time Sam got there. There was a beautiful waterfall cascading down the mountainside. The white water created a layer of foam as it roared over the dark shale-like rock. All of them headed over for a drink of the crystal clear water. Sam was actually becoming used to quenching his thirst this way. After he had his fill, he sat by the waterfall gazing upward. The mountain towered up into the clouds, further than he could see.

"Amazing, isn't it," Bakari commented as he sat down by Sam. "Have you ever seen a more beautiful mountain than this?"

Sam shook his head. "How could we possibly climb that far up?"

"You ask too many questions," Chelsea replied before Bakari could answer. Sam hadn't noticed her join them while he was staring in awe up toward the top. "Let's go find out if we can or not. You are not afraid to try, are you?" she added with a playful smile.

"Of course not," he said with an incredulous look on his face. "I am ready to go all the way up to the very top." He hoped his confident answer would mask the doubts that he was trying to hide.

Juan jumped up from his resting place under a large maple tree. "Let's go already!" he shouted in excitement as he took off up the base of the mountain.

Marveling at the energy and stamina of his companions, Sam pushed himself to keep up with them. Despite giving his all, he found himself lagging behind everyone else. There seemed to be a trail up the mountainside that the group was following. The girl that Sam hadn't met yet looked behind her to see how far away he was from the group. She stopped and waited for him to catch up.

"How can you guys go so far without even taking a break?" Sam panted while he attempted to catch his breath.

"Don't worry. We'll take one soon. There is a perfect resting spot up ahead."

"So you have climbed it before?" he questioned.

"Only a few times. But there is always something new to discover. I'm Masika. I am very pleased to meet you. Shall we see if we can gain some ground?"

"Sure," groaned Sam as he tried to force himself to move his body at a faster pace. As he watched Masika cover ground with ease, he noticed that she too had the agility and strength of an athlete. It struck him that he probably was the only nonathletic one here. It also made him realize that being good at a sport didn't automatically make you arrogant and cruel as he had assumed. So much for stereotypes.

Masika and Sam caught up with the others at the resting spot. Sam couldn't believe what he was seeing. On each side of the path were trees laden with fruit. There was a tree with big juicy apples, inviting him to take a bite. Next to it, grew a tree full of bananas, ripe and ready to be picked. Nearby, a tree of deliciously perfect oranges hung down tantalizingly. The parade of fruit trees continued with perfectly shaped pears growing alongside the oranges. Mouths watering at the sight, everyone went to grab their favorite fruit. Sam decided on an apple and sat down next to Chelsea and Juan. Taking a huge bite, he savored the sweet flavor as it lingered in his mouth. While the entire group sat silently enjoying the treat, Sam tried to calculate how much longer the climb would take them. He wondered how long they had before darkness descended on them. Maybe they would be heading back soon. Looking up at the sky to try to gauge how much daylight they had left, he searched to find the sun but couldn't find it anywhere. Yet it was bright out like the middle of a cloudless summer day. He also marveled at the fact that while the mountain had appeared to be steep and imposing, the trail up had been manageable, even for him.

Chelsea's voice snapped him out of his thoughts back into reality, if that is what this really was. "No questions yet?"

"Nothing but questions," he answered back. "None of this makes any sense."

"That's where your problem is," answered Juan. "Don't try to make any sense of it. Just enjoy the journey." With that Juan jumped up and started the climb once again. Determined not to fall behind, Sam quickly followed.

Despite his best efforts, Sam once again found himself trailing everyone else. As he struggled to draw nearer, he found Chelsea waiting for him. "Your turn to babysit me?"

"No, it's not like that at all. We just want to make sure you don't get lost. All of us have been on this trail before except you. Besides, I enjoy your company." She studied him a minute. "Are you having fun?"

Without thinking he replied, "Much more than I was before you joined me." His face turned red as he instantly regretted his hasty reply. "I'm sorry, I shouldn't have said that."

Chelsea laughed. "I'm not offended at all. In fact, it is kind of flattering."

Together, they continued the climb toward the summit. As they came closer to the top, Sam heard a rustling sound up ahead. It had to be one of their climbing partners. Excited to see the others, he raced in the direction the unfamiliar sound was coming from. He suddenly froze in his tracks.

"What's the matter?" Chelsea asked with a puzzled expression.

Without moving, he answered with a frightened whisper. "There's a mountain lion up ahead."

Chelsea surveyed the area a moment. "Yep, you're right," she observed, showing no concern at all.

The color drained from Sam's face. With panic showing in his eyes, he pleaded with Chelsea to find a solution to their dilemma. She let out a shrill whistle, and the mountain lion responded by running right at them. Seeing Sam's expression, she shouted out as the big cat got to within ten feet. "Sit, Whiskers." The mountain lion obeyed. "Don't worry, he's friendly. Matter of fact, so are all the animals here." She moved forward and began petting it like it was a housecat. "Whiskers wouldn't have been my choice for a name, but I wasn't the first to meet him. Would you like to pet him too? He likes to be scratched on his head."

"No, thanks. I think I'll pass," said Sam as he attempted to breathe normally again.

After their encounter with Whiskers, they finally caught up with the rest of the group. "Stop at this spot over here," called out Juan.

From the location he was standing, you could see clearly for miles. Sam stood and soaked in the majesty of the mountain and the surrounding valley. He had never seen a more beautiful view in his life. A refreshing breeze softly blew across his face. Again, he was aware that despite the fact that no sun could be seen, it didn't seem any later than when they had begun the climb.

"When are we heading back down?" he asked Juan.

"As soon as we make it to the top."

"But isn't it going to get dark?"

"No, it most definitely won't be getting dark before we finish. Why do you ask? Do you have somewhere you need to be?" Juan and Bakari looked at each other in amusement.

"No, I guess I don't."

"Well then, get yourself ready for the most amazing scenery you have ever seen."

As they headed up near the summit, Sam began to hear a slight ringing sound. He searched for the origin of the noise but saw nothing. Somehow, it was familiar to him, but he couldn't seem to place it. Finally, he realized that it was his alarm going off. The mountain and the faces of his friends disappeared and were replaced by his bedroom. Sam slammed the alarm clock off in a fit of rage. Discouraged that he couldn't finish his adventure, he slowly got up and headed to the bathroom to take a shower. He wished that this world could be as wonderful as his dream world. Shaking his head in frustration, he let the water spray over him while he pondered his latest dream. What was really going on? He had no logical explanation for any of it. Regardless, he needed to get ready for another day at school.

Sam had more trouble focusing in class than usual. His head swirled with questions. Why was he having these dreams? What was this place that he went to the last two nights? Who were these kids, and where did they come from? Would he be transported again tonight to this strange but wonderful world? Forcing himself to concentrate, he made it to lunchtime without allowing his thoughts to drift away from him. He found an unoccupied spot away from the crowd and started to open his lunch.

"Mind if I keep you company?"

He saw Valerie standing near him. His heart began to pound out of his chest. Trying to keep his nervousness hidden, he smiled at her. "No, I don't mind at all."

"I wasn't sure if you wanted to be alone or not," said Valerie as she set her lunch down next to his.

"You can sit by me anytime you want." Sam felt himself blush. Was that an incredibly dumb thing to say or what? She probably thinks I'm so lame. Valerie pretended not to notice his embarrassment.

"Thanks," she said as she sat down.

Sam tried not to stare at her as she bowed her head to pray before she started eating. She was absolutely gorgeous. She had long red hair and green eyes that sparkled with energy and radiated joy. *Why would a girl like that come and sit by me?* Sam wondered.

"You look like you want to say something but don't quite dare. Go ahead, ask me anything. I promise, I don't bite."

"Okay," said Sam hesitantly. "Why are you being friendly to me? Most people treat me like the plague."

"I'm not most people, Sam. I happen to like someone who can be himself regardless of what anyone else thinks. Most of the kids here are so busy trying to be popular that they don't even know who they are anymore. Everyone seems to think putting on some kind of act will make others like them. And besides that, I enjoy reading too," she said with a grin. "I even read The Phantom Narratives series."

When Sam got home that evening, his mom had already left for work. He whistled to himself as he began his almost daily ritual of searching for a meal that he could make. He had begun to cook a little bit out of necessity. At least he could vary his meals a little bit this way. Unfortunately, the refrigerator and cupboards were almost bare. His mood began to sour with his discovery. His mom had been skipping meals due to her relationship with Ken.

"Just because you want to lose weight doesn't mean I shouldn't have a little food to eat," he muttered. He finally found a few slices of stale bread to make toast with. After finishing his homework, he thought about starting on some of his mom's project list so he would have a little more time to relax this weekend. Instead, he spent the rest of his night reading. As he got ready for bed, his mind drifted off to his lunchtime with Valerie. Was this the start of a relationship or just a friendship? Either way, he enjoyed her company. It didn't hurt to have a friend at school to make the day go a little better. He envisioned her sitting next to him in the lunch room as he went to sleep. He didn't even think about what the night would bring.

Sam felt something tickling his nose. He tried to brush it away, but it stayed where it was. Irritated, he opened his eyes to see what was interfering with his sleep. He found himself lying in tall grass that was gently swaying with the wind. The tips of the blades were brushing back and forth across his face. As he got up from the ground, he slowly looked around to get his bearings. Once again, the terrain was unfamiliar. He hadn't a clue what to do next. Panic should have been setting in by now, but Sam felt a sense of peace. There was nothing about this place that felt threatening at all. In the distance, across from where he was standing, was a huge desert. Sand with a slight reddish hue covered the ground as far as Sam could see. The landscape was broken up by magnificent trees with various fruit on them, identical to the ones that were on the mountain. Bright cactus glistened in the radiant light, showing off unusual colors, among them pink, blue, and orange. Some shades were so unique that there wasn't anything to compare them to. Sam finally turned to his right when a rustling noise broke the silence.

"I see you have awakened. I hope your rest was a peaceful one." It was the voice of Hatsuko, the Japanese girl he had met earlier. She was sitting under a flowering tree of some type with a book in her hand. "You may join me if you would like."

Sam walked over slowly, still gazing at the vast desert. He suddenly became aware of the fact that she held a real book in her hand. "You read here too?"

"Of course we do," she said with a gentle laugh. "Everything you have in your world is available here in its perfected form. This also means that anything that did not have any good in it has been eliminated." She paused as if she was unsure how to say what came next. "I know you have many questions about this world, and why you are here. Everything will be revealed to you in the proper time. Until then, please don't try to understand everything. It will be much more enjoyable for you on your visits. Currently, this is not your home. It will be someday, but now is not the time."

"May I ask at least a few questions?" he asked hesitantly.

"Of course," she laughed. "But I reserve the right to not answer."

"Are we going to hike the desert today?"

"Do you see Juan coming up behind us?" she responded.

He turned and scanned the area. "No, I don't see anyone."

"Then the answer is no. I would much rather stay here." She looked at Sam and gave him a shy smile. "Isn't this a beautiful spot to enjoy the scenery?"

Sam nodded. The two of them sat in silence, not in an awkward or uncomfortable way, but as two friends relaxing together without the pressure of having to say anything at all. All his problems and worries seem to melt away. He couldn't remember a time that he felt as at peace with who he was as a person than he did right now. He sat and soaked in the serene setting.

Smiling, he turned toward Hatsuko. She had disappeared. He jumped up and started to run. He didn't know which way to run, but he did it anyway, calling out her name as he went. The ground started to shake, and Sam felt his body tossed from side to side. Everything had disappeared into a hazy darkness. A bright light broke through the black, and he saw his mom's face inches from his. She was shaking him, trying to get him to wake up. He screamed in fright.

His mom backed up quickly with a confused expression. "Sam, I really need to get some sleep. You keep yelling out about a hat or something." She glanced at the clock with a disoriented gaze. "Don't you need to get up for school anyway?"

He quickly checked the time and, in one fluid motion, leaped out of bed and rushed toward the bathroom. After closing the door, he ran back in to his room. "Just go back to bed, Mom. You were sleepwalking again."

As he was heading to school on his bike, he tried to make some sense of what was happening to him, but he could not begin to fathom why every time he slept, he somehow woke up in a different world. He also wondered why that world seemed so perfect, and this one seemed so messed up. He found himself longing more and more to go back to his other world and all his friends. A cloud of depression came over him as he parked his bike and locked it up. With a sigh he headed into the building. Maybe he would see Valerie again today. Then this world wouldn't be quite as hard to tolerate.

When he entered the building, he saw a man he hadn't met before standing near the door. As soon as he spotted Sam, his face lit up with a big smile. It was as if he was waiting for Sam to show up. He must have recently graduated from college by his youthful appearance. The black beard was neatly trimmed, and his hair styled perfectly. His muscles bulged from under his shirt. As the man strode toward him, Sam quickly realized who he was and the purpose of their upcoming introduction. It wasn't the first time he encountered a basketball coach intent on recruiting him for the team.

"Hello, Sam," the man said with a wide smile. "I'm Mr. Gordon, varsity basketball coach here. I was told about a tall freshman we would be having in our ranks this year."

"I guess that would explain how you knew my name. Pleased to meet you, sir," said Sam as he extended his hand.

"I am very impressed, Sam. Most boys your age are not quite as well-mannered as you. I can tell you wouldn't be a discipline problem. I already have enough of those on the team," he said with a laugh. Noticing that Sam was concerned about the time, he offered to walk with him to his next class. "We have a pretty good group of players in our school, but none of them have much height. If we got you in the weight room and strengthened that body of yours, you could really help us in the future. A little basketball experience with the junior varsity would make a big difference also."

"I'm flattered that you would consider me for your team, sir, but I really hate basketball."

"Sam, think about it this way. Imagine playing in the big game with everyone cheering for you, including a cute red-headed girl. Think about making the winning basket or blocking the other team's final shot. You would be a big man on campus, pun intended." He laughed heartily at his own joke. "How much would you hate basketball then? Just think about it for a while before you give me an answer."

He gave Sam a big slap on the back. As he walked away, he turned around. "Oh, and start eating about five meals a day. You are way too scrawny right now." With a wave of the hand, he disappeared down the hall.

At lunchtime, Sam found himself a spot as far away from everyone as he could. He waited anxiously to see if Valerie would find him again. Just as he was about to give up, he spotted her heading his way. He tried taking deep breaths to help him appear calm.

"Hey, Sam. Congratulations on joining the basketball team."

Sam gave her an incredulous look. "Where did you hear that from?"

"My biology teacher, Mr. Randolph, is also the junior varsity basketball coach. I overheard him talking to Mr. Gordon about a tall freshman that was joining the team. They seemed pretty excited about it. They evidently have high hopes for you."

"If they saw me play, they might feel differently," he answered wryly.

"I'm sure you will do great," said Valerie reassuringly.

"We should start eating," Sam said in an attempt to change the subject. He watched again as she bowed her head to pray.

When she finished praying, she saw Sam quickly turn his head away. "You realize that you were staring at me, don't you?"

Embarrassed, he confessed the reason for his rudeness. "I wish I had enough guts to pray at school. I'm a Christian, but I guess I'm too afraid of drawing attention to myself."

"I understand how you feel," she said sympathetically, "but what others think really doesn't matter. It's what God wants that is important."

"I know that you're right, but sometimes it's hard to do."

"What church do you go to?" she asked.

"I go to Riverton Community Church with my Uncle Jason, when he's not working out of town."

"What do you do when he isn't around?"

"I have to either ride my bike or stay home. My mom always says she is going to go, but when Sunday comes, she makes up some kind of an excuse."

"You could come with my family if you need a ride sometime. We go to the Baptist church in West Logansville."

Sam's heart started beating harder. "Thanks for the offer. That sounds great."

Too soon for Sam, lunchtime drew to a close. He guessed that he was now a basketball player. He would rather do that than disappoint Valerie.

Sam arrived home to find his mom watching television. "You must have tonight off."

"Yes, I do, and I definitely deserve it. I'm going to sit here all night long and do nothing."

"Sounds exciting," Sam said sarcastically.

She ignored Sam's comment. "If you have anything else to say, do it now. My judge show starts in five minutes."

"Hey, Mom, do we have a basketball anywhere?"

"No, why would we? You hate basketball. Come to think of it, so do I. It reminds me of watching your father play in school. What a waste of time that turned out to be. You have his height and my athletic ability. Unfortunately for you, that isn't the best mix. Life isn't fair," she said with a big sigh.

"I would agree with that," said Sam. "So what do we have for supper?"

"Beats me. I'm dieting, you know. There might be some bologna in the fridge. Oh, it's time for my show."

"Nice talking to you, Mom. I'll be in the kitchen fixing myself a gourmet five-course meal."

"Okay, have fun," she said, distracted by her program.

After gulping down his bologna sandwich, Sam decided to head over to the elementary school near his house. Maybe some kid had forgotten to bring a ball in after recess. He rode his bike around to the back of the school to find the basketball hoops. Two young boys were playing on one side while the rest of courts were unoccupied. Scouring the area with his eyes, he noticed that there was a ball lying in the weeds. He couldn't believe his luck. Carefully setting down his bike, he bent over and picked up the ball. When was the last time he had shot a basketball?

He dribbled awkwardly a couple of times, then put up a shot that totally missed everything. After he retrieved it, he decided to move a little closer. At least until he got warmed up. His next shot clanked off the backboard without hitting the rim. He looked back nervously at the two boys. They didn't seem to notice. Trying again, he bounced one off the front of the rim. Satisfied that he was improving, he went back to the same spot to shoot. This time the ball rolled around the rim and finally went in. He pumped his fist in the air and gave a soft cry of victory. Then he noticed the other side of the court had grown silent. The boys were slowly making their way toward him. Had they seen his excitement over making a short little jump shot? He supposed he would soon find out.

The boys stared at him quietly for a moment. The shorter of the two, a dark-haired boy with glasses, spoke first. "You sure are tall," he said in wonder. "Are you an NBA player?"

"Not yet," Sam said stifling a laugh. "Time for me to get going," he declared as he headed toward his bike.

"Hey, mister," said the other boy, "can you dunk a ball before you go?"

Sam tried to quickly think of an excuse. "I had better not do that here. I might tear down the rim and ruin this basket. You wouldn't want me to do that, would you?"

Both boys nodded their heads. Sam thought he had saved himself some embarrassment, but the second boy was persistent. "Then can you at least make a basket?"

Not knowing how to escape this one, he reluctantly agreed. He took the ball and started walking over to the basket. "No, mister. Shoot it from over here."

He looked at how far away they were. He had no realistic chance of making it. Nevertheless, he had to try. He dribbled once and put up a shot. It missed everything by at least ten feet. The boy with the glasses ran to retrieve it. The other boy asked him if he could stay until he made one. Grumbling beneath his breath, Sam nodded. He missed the next ten shots with only one being close at all.

"All of us big guys are only used to shooting at close range," he explained. He dribbled slowly to within five feet of the hoop, putting up a shot as he prayed to God quietly that he would make one. It bounced hard off the backboard. With determination, he put up three more shots. The last one swished through the net. Relief flooded over him. "Sorry guys, I have to go."

As he went to grab his bike, he heard the boy with the glasses say to his friend, "I told you he wasn't an NBA player."

"You were right," the other boy responded. "He stinks."

Sam peddled away as fast as he could. The boy was right. How was he ever going to be able to impress Valerie when he was so incredibly bad?

When Sam walked through the garage door, he could see his mom dozing on the couch. He tried to make it to his room to do his homework without disturbing her. Then he wouldn't have to tell her where he had been. Just when he thought he had been successful, her eyes popped open. "Hey, Sam. I must have dozed off. Are you just getting home?"

"Yes, Mom. I'm heading up to do my homework."

"Wait a minute, Sam. Come talk to me." Reluctantly, he came and sat down. "*Dancing with the Stars* is coming on now. I love how graceful the dancers are." She sighed loudly. "I wish that I was that beautiful."

"You're pretty good looking for an older lady," Sam commented, trying to make her feel better.

"Thanks, I think," she said with a grin.

"Why do they call this *Dancing with the Stars*? Most of them are has-beens trying to resurrect their careers," he complained. "And how come they hardly wear any clothes? Does someone have to be half-naked to be a good dancer?"

"I don't mind it at all. There are some hunks that look pretty appealing with their shirts off," she replied.

Sam was repulsed by her comment. "Mom, don't be gross. That's totally disgusting! Can I go do homework now?"

"Sure," she said. "It's your loss."

Sam couldn't believe how fortunate he was. If he told her that he was on the team, he would have to explain why he had a sudden change of heart about playing basketball. He would have to tell her the truth at some point, but at least he had time to think it through. Besides, why do it now when he could wait until later. He got out his school books and began to finish the things that were due tomorrow, hurrying through his work so he could go to bed early. Maybe then, he could spend more time in his other world, if he did go there again tonight. His adventures had begun just a few short days ago, but deep inside his soul, it seemed somehow familiar, as if he had always known of its existence. Maybe he had.

The sound of water gently flowing down its intended path soothed Sam as he slept. He could recognize the sound of a tide hitting the shoreline in the distance. Memories of vacationing at a cottage when he was young surfaced from deep in his memory where he had hidden them. Back when his parents were still together, and life was uncomplicated and carefree–at least in his eyes. Before endless arguing and yelling had replaced laughter and happy times. Sam was young then, about five years old, when his dad had moved away. He promised Sam that he would still be around, but he never came back. That was the only thing Sam could remember from his life when he had a real family. Somehow, he must not have been good enough to prevent the breakup. Feelings of rejection burned like an out-of-control fire in his brain, destroying everything in its path. Sam fought to block out the negative images that could destroy him if he let them. The past must remain buried where it belonged, never to resurface again.

After listening to the tranquil sound of the water for some time, Sam started to stir. Suddenly, he felt wet all over his body. He woke up immediately, searching for the water's source. He heard laughter behind him and quickly turned to see Juan, Chelsea, and Bakari standing there.

"We were waiting for you to wake up," said Juan with a smile. "Chelsea suggested we help the process along a little."

Chelsea shrugged her shoulders as Sam gave her a glare. As Sam looked around, he could see a small brook meandering down a hillside, emptying into a large lake. "What do you three have planned today?" asked Sam with suspicion written all over his face. "Sailing across the ocean or skydiving without a parachute?"

"We don't have an ocean here," Bakari said. "All the water we have flows down from the Great City," he explained.

"I personally think the skydiving idea sounds good," added Juan.

"Wait a minute," Sam said with surprise registering on his face. "There are cities here?"

"Of course, silly," Chelsea said playfully. "Where do you think everyone lives?"

"I guess I hadn't really thought about it," Sam answered sheepishly.

"We all have houses specially made for us. The Master Builder makes one for each of us. All we have to do is supply the building material," Chelsea offered.

Before Sam could ask another question, several more kids appeared. Some of them Sam hadn't met yet, but he did see a few familiar faces, including Masika and Hatsuko. Sam wondered what was going to happen next. It was sure to be something completely new to him.

While the group chatted amongst themselves, Sam pulled Hatsuko aside. "Do you know what we are going to do?"

"Yes, however, you always have a choice whether or not you participate. Many times, I prefer to just watch. It is enjoyable to me to be with my friends even when I am not doing the same thing they are. Today's activity involves diving to the bottom of the lake and exploring what exists down there."

"But where is the scuba gear?" said Sam with a bewildered expression.

"There is none. It is not necessary."

"Is that even safe?" he questioned.

"There is no danger at all," she said reassuringly.

"But how do you breathe underwater?"

"You just do, Sam."

Somehow, he believed that what she said was true. In this place, the impossible seemed to happen with regularity. He watched Chelsea and Juan talk excitedly about the upcoming dive. Turning to Hatsuko, he asked, "Are Chelsea and Juan dating?"

Hatsuko gave him an understanding look. "No, we don't date or get married here."

"Why not, Hatsuko?"

"Remember that everything here is a better version of your world. Dating can be full of hardships and pain along with good times. Marriages can regretfully end up in divorce. The King is the only bridegroom we will ever need. That is all I can say right now."

Sam put his hands on his head. "I'm so confused."

"It will all become clear in time. Please trust me when I say this," said Hatsuko in a gentle tone.

"Sam!" hollered Juan, "it's time to dive."

"Go ahead, have fun exploring," she said encouragingly. "I enjoyed our conversation very much. I will watch the diving from here."

"I trust Hatsuko explained what we are going to do," Juan said with a huge grin on his face. "Chelsea offered to be your dive partner.

That way, you won't need to worry about where to go or feel like you have to keep up with everyone, especially me." With that, he ran headlong down toward the lake and dove in to the water. Bakari, Masika, and the rest of kids assembled there followed close behind.

Chelsea approached him, smiling happily. "You're not still mad at me for interrupting your beauty sleep, are you?"

"Of course not. I wouldn't want to miss all the fun. I do have a question though."

"I'm sure you do," she replied, pretending to be exasperated by rolling her eyes. "Go ahead, but only one. We need to join the others."

"How come nobody changed into bathing suits? Won't we need dry clothes when we're done?"

As they walked to the edge of the lake, Chelsea gave him an answer. "When we get out, our clothes will quickly become dry. Don't try to understand."

"So let me get this straight. If one of us fell in the water, we would become instantly dry when we got out."

"Not instantly, but very quickly."

Sam nodded with understanding, then without warning, shoved Chelsea into the water. Before he could move, she grabbed his leg and pulled him under. With smiles on their faces, they began to swim toward the bottom of the picturesque lake.

It was nothing like any lake he had ever heard of. It was teeming with creatures swimming back and forth, many of which should not have existed in a freshwater setting. There was every kind of fish that he could have imagined and many beyond his wildest dreams. He swam next to translucent jellyfish, watching eels and swordfish as they floated by. There was even a creature that had fins and gills like a fish but also had wings and feathers. As he followed Chelsea deeper, he almost forgot that he shouldn't have been able to breathe underwater like he was doing right now. He felt no fear, trusting Chelsea completely. When they finally reached the bottom, brightly colored coral came into focus as it jutted out from the lake's floor. Sea plants swayed with every movement the two of them made. Crabs scuttled along the ground, competing with sea urchins for hiding places. Two dolphins swam close to them, startling Sam for a moment. They appeared to be smiling as they drew nearer in a seemingly friendly manner. One eventually came up alongside of Sam, nuzzling him with its nose, while the other followed Chelsea. Reaching out her hand, she gently stroked the dolphin's back. Sam followed her lead and did the same with the dolphin nearest him. The two dolphins contentedly stayed near them as they explored the rocky bottom. Every fish, plant, and living thing was seemingly perfect. Strange lake fish combined with ocean dwellers to create a type of magical aquarium. Out of the corner of his eye, Sam noticed a dark large figure heading in his direction. Terror seized him when he realized what it was. A very large shark swiftly approached the spot where he and Chelsea were swimming.

Sam frantically waved his arms to get Chelsea's attention, but she was oblivious to the upcoming danger. The rest of their friends were nowhere in sight. He swam as fast as he was able over to Chelsea and grabbed her arm. Turning around, she spotted the shark. A huge grin spread over her face as she anticipated the shark's arrival. Confused by her reaction, a panicked Sam searched the lake floor for a cave or some type of hiding spot. Finding nowhere to go, he got as close to Chelsea as he could. Maybe together they could fight off an attack. Without warning, Chelsea swam toward the shark. When it reached her, she opened her arms wide and gave it a huge hug. Sam started to relax, remembering the incident with the mountain lion. Finally it swam away, apparently satisfied with Chelsea's show of affection. After a lengthy exploration, Chelsea signaled for Sam to follow her to the surface. Many of the divers were already there sharing their exploits underwater.

"That was awesome!" Chelsea shouted as she plopped down on the ground.

Sam sat down beside her. "Except for our encounter with the shark, which scared me half to death, by the way."

"You are so lucky," said a boy who happened to overhear them. "I didn't get to see the shark today." The boy continued talking, but his voice became garbled, and Sam couldn't comprehend what he was trying to say. Everything started to fade until the lakeside scene totally disappeared.

⎯⎯•⎯⎯

Sam woke up in his bed. He laid there trying to digest everything that had just happened. Within a minute, his alarm went off. He slowly gathered his thoughts and began his daily ritual of preparing for another school day. After getting dressed, he hopped on his bike for the short ride to school. Soon, the weather would turn too cold to ride, so he wanted to take advantage of any opportunity he had to use it. When he got to school, he rode over to the bike rack. As he was locking up his bike, a large hand grabbed him and spun him around. It was Josh. He was quite a bit shorter than Sam but outweighed him by at least fifty pounds. He was built like a brick wall and was as friendly as an upset pit bull.

He pointed his finger at Sam. "I have a message for your little girlfriend. You tell her nobody gets away with disrespecting me. I don't care if she is a girl. She has a lesson to learn, and I am going to be the one to give it to her. As for you, stay out of my way, or you will need a face transplant. Understand?"

"Yes, you've made it quite clear." Josh gave him a threatening stare before turning and entering the building. Sam shook his head. This day was not getting off to a good start.

As if concentrating while he was in class hadn't been hard enough before with everything that was going on in Sam's life, Josh's threats made it almost impossible to keep his focus. He needed to let Valerie know about what just happened. What did Josh have planned, and how could he be stopped? The answer to those questions eluded Sam no matter how often they popped into his mind during his morning classes. After a long morning, lunchtime finally arrived. He made his way to his usual spot in the farthest corner of the lunchroom. He anxiously scanned the room for Valerie. He checked his phone, but there were no messages. He kept glancing at the time while he searched the crowd for a glimpse of her red hair.

A voice from behind him startled Sam. "Who are you waiting for?" Valerie asked as she observed him glancing at the main entrance to the lunch room.

"What took you so long, and why are you coming in through that door?" he demanded.

Valerie gave him an irritated look. "You don't own me, in case you didn't know. I can come in when I want and through any door I choose. In fact, I don't even have to sit right here."

"I'm sorry, but I was worried about you."

Valerie's face registered her anger. "You're scaring me with your possessiveness. It's not like we're engaged or even dating. I just thought it would be nice to have a friend that liked books as much as me. For your information, I was discussing the newest book releases with Miss Collins. I thought maybe I could talk to you about some of them, but maybe I will just find another spot to eat." She got up from her chair.

"Valerie, wait," he pleaded. "I have an important message to give you. Please sit back down." Reluctantly she gave in and returned to her chair. "This morning, Josh found me by the bike rack and told me that he was going to get back at you for what you said to him. I was afraid that he had already done something to you. I'm sorry if I offended you."

Her irritation melted away, replaced by remorse. "I guess I owe you an apology too. I have a temper, in case you didn't already know. Thanks for making me aware. I'll be careful to stay out of his way, but I am not going to live in fear. That's the response he wants to get from me. I am not going to give him the satisfaction."

"Are we still friends?" Sam asked timidly.

"Of course we are." She paused for a moment. "You will never guess who is coming out with a new novel," she said with excitement. "We can talk about it while we eat." Sam smiled in relief as he opened up his lunch.

When Sam got home, he found his mom getting ready for work. "Sam, I have some news for you," she said with an excited smile. "This Friday night, I am inviting Ken and his son for dinner."

"He has a son? I guess I never pictured him as the fatherly type."

"Well, he is a father, regardless of how you picture him. I don't know much about his son because we have never met. Ken shares custody with his ex-wife."

"Do I have to be there?" asked Sam with an annoyed expression.

"Of course you do. It would be awkward for his son without you there."

"Wonderful," said Sam sarcastically. "I'm going to start my homework now." He bounded up the stairs two at a time before his mom had a chance to lecture him about his attitude. Tomorrow night was not going to be one of the best nights of his life. The worst part was that he could do absolutely nothing to make it better.

While he was working on his homework, his mind began to drift. When he thought about swimming underwater, it was just too incredible to believe. How could any of this be happening? Somehow, it seemed nothing at all like a dream. For all he knew, that was the real world. Thinking about it too much made his head hurt. Logic did not seem to apply to this situation. He decided he needed to stop trying to figure it all out, so instead of staying up trying to make all the pieces fit together, he got ready for bed early. Nevertheless, he couldn't help but wonder if he would journey once again to his other world. How long could this continue? There just weren't any solid answers but plenty of questions.

Sam awoke to sounds of horses. He found himself in the middle of a pasture with horses grazing nearby. Alarmed that he was on the ground right next to such large animals, he quickly got up and brushed off his clothes.

"Well, I see you've discovered what we are going to do for our next adventure."

He turned and saw Juan standing there. "So we're eating grass for fun?"

"Much better than that, my sarcastic friend. A group of us are going to go horseback riding."

"Where is everyone else?"

"They must have decided that it was too far to run the whole way," Juan said with a grin on his face. "Only Bakari can keep up with me, and he is doing something else today."

The rest of the riders began to arrive. Sam recognized the goalie from the soccer game as he walked up with a Russian boy whose name he couldn't remember. Others appeared that Sam had never met. It constantly amazed him that it seemed as if every nationality was represented. It was then that he realized everyone understood each other, and they all got along. His eyes lit up when he saw Hatsuko appear. He felt a connection to her somehow, not in a physical way, but as someone who shared a kindred spirit. Maybe they could ride together. It would make learning how to ride much more fun.

"Hi, Sam. I trust you are well today."

"I'm better now that you are here."

Hatsuko gave him a quizzical look. "Is there some sort of problem?"

"I'm afraid so," he said hesitantly. "I have never ridden a horse before. I don't want anybody to laugh," he admitted with embarrassment. "I know you won't make fun of me if I fall off or do something stupid."

"Everyone has been a novice at some point," Hatsuko reassured him. "There is not a person here that would mock you for trying to learn. Arrogance has no place in this world. However, if you would prefer that I teach you, I would be honored to do so."

"Yes, I definitely would like that very much," he said with a relieved expression on his face.

"Come, let's go find our horses."

"So how do we decide which one to ride?"

"All of us have a favorite here. Mine is that handsome black stallion up to your left. His name is Shadow. Let's see if I can find the one that you will be riding." Hatsuko scanned the area for a moment before spotting Sam's horse. Starting toward it, she motioned for Sam to follow her. Off in the distance, he could see a unique looking horse that had multiple colors on its body. "This mare is Rainbow. She is very gentle so you do not have to be afraid of her. Shall we give it a try?"

Sam nodded his head. "I'm ready," he said with determination.

Hatsuko pointed toward a spot to her right. "You will find our saddles over there."

They both grabbed one off the ground and headed over to their horses. Hatsuko showed Sam how to put it on Rainbow before saddling Shadow. After a few tries, Sam managed to stay on Rainbow's back.

"Good job, Sam. I think you are going to get the hang of this very quickly," Hatsuko said encouragingly. She patiently gave him instructions on what to do. Sam could feel himself relax as they slowly started off with Hatsuko leading the way.

"Where are we going?" he hollered out.

She turned her head toward him and smiled. "You will see soon enough. Just enjoy the journey to our destination."

Sam looked around. There were no other riders to be seen. Only a beautiful blue sky and breathtaking scenery to gaze at in every direction. Brightly colored birds sang their songs, and small animals darted into their hiding places, with an occasional glance at the passing horses. After climbing a large hill, Hatsuko stopped her horse. Sam soon caught up and brought Rainbow to a stop next to her. On the other side of the hill was a valley with houses spread across the countryside.

"This is where some of us live. Do you want to see my house?"

Sam nodded as he tried to take it all in. Side by side, they started off together into the valley.

As they drew nearer to the homes, Sam marveled at the architecture. It was unlike anything he had ever seen. Each house had a unique design and shape to it. The material used for constructing them was definitely not wood, and no type of siding was used. Instead, it shone like a type of precious metal unknown to him. All the structures had a different version of stone or perhaps metal. Every one was quite stunning in its own right.

"Who built all these houses?" asked Sam in awestruck wonder.

"The Master Builder created each and every one. They are custom designed for each person living here."

"How could one person possibly have the time and resources to handle such a massive undertaking?"

"The Master Builder is not like any builder you have in your world. Everything He needs is at His command."

Sam pondered her statement. Unable to fully comprehend her explanation, he decided to leave it alone for now. "Is your house nearby?"

"We are very close. Do you see the pink-tinted stones on the house to your right? That one is mine. Would you like to come inside?"

"If you don't mind, I would love to see it."

"All right then, let's head in that direction."

They soon arrived at Hatsuko's house. She stopped under a shade tree alongside a magnificent flower garden. Dismounting, she signaled for Sam to do the same. "Just leave Rainbow under the tree."

After almost falling getting out of the saddle, he questioned the wisdom of not tying up the horses. "Won't they run away if we let them roam free?"

"Don't worry, they would never do that. Let's go inside."

"Do you live here all alone?"

"Yes, this is my own accommodation."

"Where is your family?"

Hatsuko smiled. "One of my family members is standing right beside me. All the others you have met so far are part of my family also."

"I'm honored that you would think of me as family, but I am talking of a biological family."

"That is exactly what I am talking about also. All who live here are brothers and sisters of mine."

Her answer perplexed Sam, but he also was aware that there were things happening here that he just couldn't comprehend yet. Upon entering the house, Sam looked in all directions, trying to take in the beauty of it. "How can you afford a place like this?"

"I do have a job, but this home was given to me. Every one of these houses was freely given to us, even though we did nothing to earn them. It did however come with a steep cost to the builder. You will understand this all in time. We need to head back to the horses now. Everyone else will also be returning as well."

The horses were right where they had left them. Hatsuko mounted Shadow while Sam attempted to get on the back of Rainbow. Finally, on the third try, he succeeded. After riding in silence for a while, contemplating everything he had learned and seen today, he decided to ask a few more questions.

"You mentioned that you had a job. So what is it that you do?" he asked as they traveled.

"I help out on a farm not far from here. I have always loved animals, and I enjoy taking care of them. All the jobs given out involve what you are passionate about in your world. We were created to have tasks to do even before Adam and Eve sinned. It was then that work became hard and often unpleasant."

"You are familiar with the Bible too?"

Hatsuko laughed so hard she almost fell off her horse.

"What was so funny about that?" asked Sam with embarrassment.

"I hope I did not offend you. That was not my intent at all. In answer to your question, yes, I am very familiar with it. You will find that all of us here believe in what is found in the Bible."

As they drew closer to the meadow where the horses had been grazing, Sam began to wonder what experiences would come next. Just as he was about to ask what the upcoming plans were, he suddenly found himself sitting backward in a chair in his room. Sheepishly, he got up and looked at his clock. It was set to go off any second. He turned it off and sat there for a minute, mentally drained from his busy night. With a heavy sigh, he got up to start another day.

On his way to school, he kept his eyes peeled on his surroundings, expecting Josh to appear any moment. It was almost eerie how uneventful the ride went. Parking his bike, a feeling of dread came over him. When was Josh going to strike next, and what were his plans to get his so-called revenge on Valerie? Sam vowed he would do anything to protect her like she had done for him, even if he had to take the punishment instead. After all, this mess was his fault. If he had stood up for himself instead of being a coward, Valerie wouldn't be involved. It was time to be a man and take responsibility. When he entered the door of the school, he saw a familiar face waiting for him. It was starting again.

Mr. Gordon, the varsity basketball coach, stood with crossed arms and a stoic expression on his face. To his left was a man that Sam had not met yet. He was tall, with brown hair that seemed to stay exactly in its assigned spot. A smile came to his face when he saw Sam, exposing his perfect white teeth. Sam assumed that this was Mr. Randolph, the junior varsity coach. He disliked him already. Mr. Gordon strode toward Sam confidently. Sam instantly searched for an escape route, but quickly realized he was trapped.

"Sam, good to see you this morning." Slapping him hard on the back, he motioned toward Mr. Randolph who still had a smile plastered on his face. "This is Mr. Randolph, the head coach of the junior varsity."

"Nice to meet you, Sam," he said extending his hand.

"It's a pleasure to meet you, sir."

"We were just discussing our team's chances this year when we ran into you." Mr. Gordon put his arm around Sam's shoulder. "Of course, you realize we have practice tonight after school, right?"

"No, I actually had no idea it started already."

"Basketball has become a year-long sport. Practice, conditioning, weightlifting, running, watching film–it never stops if you want to improve."

"What if I don't want to?" Both coaches stared at him. "Sorry, just attempting a joke. I had better get to class."

"So we can expect you tonight, correct?" questioned Mr. Gordon.

"Yes, sir, I will be there." Sam shook his head as hurried to his classroom. What had he gotten himself into?

Mr. Cummings roamed the front of the classroom, extoling the virtues of math and its importance in today's society. Sam tuned him out, figuring he would start listening again when he stopped rambling on about nothing of importance. Concluding that he had about ten minutes before Mr. Cummings got down to business, he let his mind wander. Too much was happening at once. He felt totally overwhelmed and confused. Then it hit him. His mom was expecting him for dinner with Kenneth and his son tonight. How long did practice last? A smile briefly crossed his face. Maybe he would have to tell Mom that he couldn't make dinner tonight. The smile disappeared as quickly as it had come. He knew how much it meant to her. As much as he didn't want to sit through the meal, he couldn't do anything to hurt her. If basketball lasted too long, he would have to tell his coach he needed to leave, which at least gave him an excuse to get out of basketball. If only he could get out of both at once.

Lunch couldn't come fast enough for Sam. It was the one thing he looked forward to at school. When he got there Valerie had already seated herself in their usual spot. "How did you get here so fast?"

"Maybe you're just slow." Sam quickly checked the time. Turning back to Valerie, he saw the grin on her face. "Sorry, I was just teasing. Miss Collins let us out a little early today."

"Why?" he wondered.

"Why not?" she answered with a shrug.

"You're more sassy than usual."

"I'll take that as a compliment," she said with a mischievous laugh. "Sassy is a good thing, right?"

"It depends," answered Sam.

"Depends on what?" She looked at him with her beautiful green eyes, expectantly awaiting his reply.

"On what person you're sassing."

"I don't think you mind too much," she declared with a twinkle in her eyes. Sam smiled as he opened up his lunch. As long as she sat with him, she could say anything she wanted to.

After school ended, he slowly headed toward the gym. Why did he let Mr. Gordon persuade him to join the team? Actually, he knew that it wasn't because of Mr. Gordon that he said yes. The real reason was that he didn't want to disappoint Valerie. For all he knew, she might like athletes, so he had better become one just in case. When he entered the gym, he saw most of the team had already arrived. All of them seemed to have basketball shorts on and were wearing fancy basketball shoes. Sam fought the urge to turn around and run out the door. Mr. Randolph noticed him standing there and came over to greet him.

"Sorry, coach, I don't have any shorts to wear. I wasn't expecting to practice tonight." He self-consciously looked down at his worn tennis shoes and his blue jeans.

"No problem," Mr. Randolph answered, brushing aside Sam's concerns. "We're just glad you came to practice. The guys are just shooting around a little bit to get warmed up. Go ahead and join them."

Reluctantly, he headed out on the floor. He decided to stay as far out on the perimeter as possible so he wouldn't have the opportunity to get many rebounds. He didn't want to shoot and get laughed at.

A short boy with glasses came over and introduced himself. "My name is Nate. Or you could call me Shrimp like the rest of the guys."

"I'm Sam, and you could call me anything you want. Just don't make any jokes about the weather."

"So you must be the star player that everyone has been looking forward to seeing."

"Actually, I'm not very good. Everyone thinks I must be because I'm tall."

A ball bounced over to where they were standing. Sam picked it up and threw it to the first person that he saw. "Don't feel bad, I'm sure that you are better than me," Nate declared. "There is no way I will ever play unless everyone else got sick."

Mr. Randolph interrupted their conversation by hollering at them. "Nate! Sam! You two need to move closer and take a few shots."

Sam could feel everyone's eyes watching him. Mr. Gordon stood near the entrance of the gym with arms folded. A ball bounced to Sam. Not knowing what to do, he nervously decided to take a couple dribbles and then take a shot. His first dribble bounced off his foot and rolled away. Not the first impression he wanted to make. The next time a ball came to him, he instantly tossed it up at the basket. It hit the rim with a clank and went off into the bleachers. Excited that he had at least hit the rim, he gave Nate a fist bump. He threw a glance over in Mr. Gordon's direction. He was nowhere to be seen.

Mr. Randolph blew his whistle for everyone to come in. "I want to start tonight by getting warmed up with a few laps around the gym. Why don't we go easy tonight. Let's do ten times around before we do some wind sprints."

Sam groaned. This was going from bad to worse. After five times around the gym, Sam was on the verge of collapse while Mr. Randolph, who was running with them, didn't even seem to be breathing hard. Sam was determined to finish all the laps along with his teammates. He had embarrassed himself enough already. He finally finished, well after the rest of his team.

"Good job, guys." Mr. Randolph said while Sam stood bent over gasping for air. "Everyone grab a drink before we start wind sprints."

Sweat poured out of Sam's body as he grabbed a drink. Nate came over by Sam and took a spot next to him. "Kind of sadistic, isn't he." Too tired to say anything, Sam nodded in agreement. This night couldn't end fast enough.

Sam limped over to his bike. He had survived his first practice. He hurt everywhere. It was time to go home and face his least favorite of all Mom's boyfriends. This was saying quite a bit, given the caliber of most of them. The bike ride home seemed longer than normal, probably because he could hardly move his legs. He parked the bike in the garage and headed inside. He knew his mom would not be happy with him. When he opened the door, he found out that he was correct.

"Sam, where have you been? I was afraid you weren't going to make it home in time. I texted you but I got no response."

Knowing he was in trouble, Sam tried to justify his actions. "Sorry, Mom. Let me explain what happened. I didn't know when I left for school that I had my first basketball practice tonight. Coach would have been disappointed if I didn't show up."

She gave him an incredulous stare. "Why did you join the basketball team? Did you change your opinion of the sport?"

"No, not really. The coaches at school have been pressuring me to try out for the team. I didn't want to disappoint them."

"So you decided to let your mother squirm instead. I can see where I stand on your list of priorities. You used to be such a considerate boy, but now you can't even text me to let me know what's going on."

"Mom, it's not like that at all. I'm sorry I forgot to text you. There's a lot going on in my life right now."

"I'm done talking about it, young man. You need to go take a shower and change into some nice clothes. I could smell you when you opened the door. Make it a quick one so you can help me set the table."

Sam came down from his shower dressed in one of his best shirts and a pair of khaki pants, hoping to get back in his mom's good graces. After setting the table, he helped in the kitchen in any way he could. He noticed with amusement that Mom was making her meatloaf again. He wished he had the heart to tell her that it was awful. Who knows, maybe it would scare Ken off. The doorbell rang.

"Sam, will you get that please."

"Sure, Mom," he hollered. When he opened the front door, he got the surprise of his life. Sam's face turned white with shock when he saw who Ken's son was.

"Well, if it isn't my old buddy from school," said Josh with a smirk. "Is your mouthy little girlfriend here to protect you?"

"So you know this nerd?" Ken snorted in disdain.

"I sure do. As a matter of fact, we have a little unfinished business together," answered Josh.

"I'll go get my mom. Have a seat anywhere." Sam hurried into the kitchen.

"How is the meal coming?"

"It will be a few more minutes. The meatloaf needs a little time in the oven yet. Why don't you go entertain the boys, and I'll bring it out soon."

"No, Mom. You have been working really hard, and I think you deserve a break. I can watch the meat. I'm sure they would much rather visit with you."

"Are you sure?" she asked with hesitation.

"Positive. If I need anything, I can call you."

Sam pondered his options. Poison the food? Or maybe escape out the back door? Finally, he came to the conclusion that he had no options at all. He looked at the meatloaf and then checked the temperature. It was as ready as it was going to be. Might as well face the inevitable. Grabbing the potholders, he took it out of the oven and brought it to the table.

"Meatloaf's ready, Mom. I'll go grab the salad." After bringing the salad and the drinks, Sam resigned himself to the fact that he would have to sit and try to converse with Ken and Josh.

"So what do you do for a living, Mr. Ken?"

After taking a big bite of meatloaf, he reluctantly mumbled, "I'm a motorcycle mechanic." He said nothing else as he continued to stuff food in his mouth.

"Sam, when you were in the kitchen, Josh was telling me that you two go to the same school. How did you meet?" asked his mom.

"I guess we just ran into each other," said Sam with a shrug of the shoulders.

Ken continued eating in silence as if he hadn't had a meal in a week. Josh on the other hand, had an expression of anguish with each bite he took. Finally, Ken put his fork down and proceeded to let out one of the loudest burps Sam had ever heard. "Good meal, babe. You got any dessert?"

"Yes, we do. I have a special surprise in the refrigerator," she said with a gleam in her eye.

Sam jumped out of his seat. "I'll go get it right now. You stay and relax, Mom."

"I'll help Sam clear the table," said Josh politely.

"What a nice gentleman you have raised, Kenny."

"Oh yeah, Josh is very gentlemanly almost all the time. Have I told you how hot you look tonight?"

Sam fought the urge to gag as he started clearing plates alongside Josh. When they went into the kitchen, Josh whispered to Sam. "That was the worst meal I've ever eaten," he said with disgust.

"Your dad seemed to like it," Sam retorted.

"He would eat dog food if you offered it to him."

"We had that last night," joked Sam.

An evil grin came across Josh's face. "If our parents get married, you and I would be brothers. I think I would like that very much."

Pretending that he hadn't heard him, Sam quickly reached into the refrigerator and took out the pie. "Josh, can you take those plates when you go back to the table?"

"Sure, anything for my soon-to-be brother."

When they entered the dining area, Ken was all ready for the next course. "What kind you got?"

"It's chocolate cream, Kenny. I know that it's your favorite," said Mom with a smile. She started to cut it into eight pieces. "Josh, do you want a piece? You didn't seem to be very hungry at supper."

"Did you make this, Mrs. Walker?"

"No, it's store bought."

"I think my appetite is returning. I might as well give it a try."

When everyone had finished eating, an uncomfortable quiet settled into the room. "I'll begin clearing the table, Mom," said Sam as he started grabbing plates.

She gave him a curious glance and then shrugged her shoulders. "When you're done in there, maybe you and Josh would like to do something together while Ken and I watch a movie. It's nice you two are such good friends."

Sam struggled to come up with a reason why that wouldn't work. While he was tossing around ideas in his mind, Josh came to the rescue. "That's very tempting, Mrs. Walker, but I already made plans with some of the guys. Dad, I'm going to head out now. We're meeting at Gabe's house."

Ken watched him move toward the door. "Hey, make sure you're in before daylight. And don't do anything I wouldn't do." He laughed as if he had made a hilarious joke.

Josh turned back from the entryway. "Don't worry, Dad. There is nothing I'm doing tonight that you wouldn't do." Grinning directly at Sam, he stepped out the door.

Sam's mom watched Josh saunter down to the sidewalk. "You should be very proud of your son, Ken. He seems like a fine young man."

Ken grabbed her hand. "Enough about him. Let's get started on the movie." They walked together into the living room. Watching them act like teenagers infatuated with each other was too much for Sam. There had to be a way to break this up. He was determined to find it, whatever the cost.

Sam finished up the homework he had for the weekend after supper. Thinking about Ken downstairs made him sick to his stomach. Should he talk to Mom after Prince Charming left for the night or wait until she had a good night's sleep? Deciding that procrastination was sometimes a valid option, he figured that it would also give him time to think of how to approach the situation tactfully. Not wanting to hurt his mom by being too blunt, he still wanted to make sure she got the message. Ken was not the man for her, nor did Sam want him for a dad. Maybe he could text his Uncle Jason. He would know just what to say. Sam could text him under the guise of wondering whether Uncle Jason was able to pick him up for church. In the course of the conversation, Sam could casually mention that Mom had an obnoxious new boyfriend with a juvenile delinquent for a son. Then Uncle Jason would give him some wise advice on how to end this relationship. Sam congratulated himself on his idea. It just might work.

Physically weary from basketball and mentally drained from their dinner party, Sam collapsed on the bed. It was a struggle just to get his clothes off and change into his pajamas. As soon as he hit the bed, he fell asleep. A distant sound echoed in Sam's head. Familiar voices but somehow different. He didn't really care who was making the sounds, he just wanted them to stop. Still groggy, he opened his eyes to find the source of his frustration. What he saw stunned him. He appeared to be in a large cave. Gigantic stalagmites and stalactites shone from the floor and ceiling. The walls glistened with unique shades of color, such as bright green and hot pink. Scanning the impressive formations on display, he found quite a few that resembled familiar animals, including a cat that appeared to be stalking a mouse. He also found a rock shaped like a table, perfectly chiseled out as if a carpenter had built it. Although there was no light source to be seen, the cavern was not dark at all. Sam noticed the talking and laughing had ceased. Silence encompassed the room, but he felt no fear. This was not a world to be afraid of, that much he had come to know.

"All right, Juan, where are you hiding?' Sam called out.

Juan trudged out from behind a rock formation. "How did you know I was here?" he asked with disappointment.

"This has the look of an adventure you might organize," Sam said with satisfaction. "Is Bakari going to materialize in a second?"

"No, but we are," called out a voice behind him, making him jump. Chelsea burst out laughing. Alongside of her with an amused grin was Masika, the girl who had climbed the mountain part of the way with him. Sam tried to give them his angriest glare, but he couldn't stop a smile from appearing on his face.

Just then, Bakari appeared. "Sorry, I'm late. Did I miss anything?"

"Nothing much, just your friends attempting to scare me to death," said Sam. "In a weird way, I'm starting to get used to it."

"That's good, because this probably won't be the last time," observed Masika.

"Who is ready to do some exploring?" said Juan excitedly.

Sam looked around warily, expecting someone else to pop out from nowhere. "Is anyone going to be joining us?"

Juan shrugged his shoulders. "You never know. We might run into somebody in one of the tunnels." Turning to address Masika, he called out to her. "Go ahead and lead the way."

Masika confidently strode to the front of the group. The section that they were in was very large, with plenty of room to walk side by side. As they walked, Sam marveled at the beauty all around him. The ceiling of the cave was probably at least ten feet high.

Sam turned to Chelsea who was walking alongside him. "How can it be so bright in here? There is no artificial lighting that I can see and enough sunlight could never get in to eliminate the darkness so completely."

Chelsea pondered the question for a few seconds as if deciding how much she should reveal to him. "You aren't going to ask questions the whole time, are you?"

"No, I promise to keep them to a minimum."

"Okay, I'm holding you to that. Otherwise, we might accidently lose you on one of the pathways while we explore." She paused to let her threat sink in. "We would eventually come back for you," she added laughingly.

Sam relaxed when he realized she was once again joking with him. Turning serious, she answered his original question. "There is no night and no darkness here. The sun does not exist either. But there is eternal light coming from our King who sits on the throne. There is no place that His light does not penetrate. Even inside of a cave."

"That makes no sense at all. What kind of a world is this?" Sam said with a perplexed look.

Again, Chelsea took a moment before answering. "You will be finding answers to all your questions very soon. Let's just enjoy the time we have right now." Sam reluctantly nodded in agreement as they walked in silence.

The spacious room started to shrink dramatically. In front of them, there was a narrow pathway that led into a tunnel. Masika guided them into the small opening. Now they had to walk single file. Sam had to duck his head in many spots as the ceiling became lower also. He began to feel a little uneasy in spite of the confidence he had in his friends. After going a short distance, the tunnel split into two separate openings heading in different directions. The right fork was the wider of the two, with a more inviting terrain. The left was significantly smaller and much rockier.

"Which way are we taking?" shouted Juan.

"When in doubt, always take the narrow road," she replied. Without hesitation, she took the left fork. No one questioned her decision, and all of them followed her lead.

Sensing Sam's unease, Chelsea sought to reassure him. "Masika knows her way around caves. Don't be concerned. She always makes the right choice."

Sam whispered back to Chelsea who was the last in line. "There aren't any lions down here, are there?"

Chelsea giggled. "Of course not, silly. What kind of world do you think this is?"

Silently hiding his embarrassment, Sam pondered her question. What kind of world did he think this was?

Deeper into the cave they went until Masika motioned for them to stop. Facing the rest of the explorers, she gave them an update on what lay ahead. "We are coming to a very small opening. To get through, we are going to have to crawl. I believe it will be well worth the trouble, and you will be glad you did."

"What are we waiting for?" shouted Juan as he and Bakari gave each other an excited glance.

Sam looked at Chelsea, hoping that she would have an objection of some sort, but she nodded approvingly. "Doesn't touching the rock ruin it by the oils released from our skin?" Sam asked.

"Not down here," Chelsea answered. "You're not trying to get out of this, are you?"

"Of course not," he said with false bravado. Knowing that it was inevitable, he reluctantly prepared himself to crawl through the hole.

With Masika leading the way, they started through the tiny crevice. Juan and Bakari slid underneath in a matter of seconds. Sam got down on the ground and shimmied his way to the other side. There were some advantages in being skinny. Right after he went through the opening, Chelsea emerged to join the others. They were in another very large open area, similar to the one they began in. Massive stalactites clung to the ceiling, improbably suspended despite their imposing size. Equally impressive stalagmites attempted to join their counterparts to create an impenetrable wall. Juan launched himself into a maze of rocks that literally glowed as if they were on fire, while Bakari silently climbed upon a large rock, unnoticed by Juan. Masika grinned as she anticipated what was to happen next. Juan came back to where she stood, searching for Bakari. Not knowing that Bakari was now up near the ceiling directly above him, Juan stopped near Masika. Before Juan was able to move again, Bakari dropped down and landed on top of him. Before Juan had a chance to collect himself, Bakari leapt to his feet and dashed down an unexplored side trail, laughing as he went. Juan charged after him threatening revenge.

Chelsea looked at Masika and rolled her eyes. "Boys must play," she said, anticipating a response from Sam.

Sam gazed at the spot Bakari had climbed. It started to turn colors before his eyes. He turned to tell Chelsea, but he saw his mom's face instead. He looked away as he rubbed his eyes and tried to focus. His mom's face reappeared. He was back in his own room.

"Sam, time to get up."

"Mom, why did you wake me? It's Saturday," he complained.

"First of all, you have a lot of projects to do today. Secondly, it's after nine already, and lastly, Jason will be here in a half hour."

Sam instantly jumped out of bed. "Why didn't you tell me earlier?" he said with annoyance.

"Just a second ago, you were upset that I was waking you. Now I didn't do it soon enough. Welcome to parenting, Elizabeth Walker."

Sam ignored her jab at him. Scrambling to find the right clothes, he banged his knee on the bedpost. Hobbling toward the bathroom, he turned back to his mom. "Why is he coming over?"

"Probably to visit with his favorite sister."

"That's not saying a lot, seeing you are his only sister."

"Well, if I did I have other sisters, I would still be his favorite."

"Why are you in such a good mood this morning, Mom?"

"Are you implying that I'm normally in a bad mood?"

"I'm not implying anything," Sam said with a smirk. He quickly closed the bathroom door to avoid the pillow that came flying his way. Both of them laughed. It was nice to have a pleasant conversation for once.

When Sam came downstairs, Uncle Jason was sitting in the living room. "How was your beauty sleep?"

"Funny man. You're definitely related to Mom." Sam plopped down beside him. "What are you doing here today?"

"It's good to see you too. Actually, since I am in town this weekend, I thought I would help you with some of your chores. I know your mom has to work tonight, so it would be a good opportunity for us to hang out together if you don't have any plans."

A gigantic smile covered Sam's face. "That would be awesome. Let's get started, Uncle Jason," he said enthusiastically.

"Why don't we eat some breakfast first," Uncle Jason said with a smile.

"I am kind of hungry," Sam admitted.

"Let's go see what we can find in the kitchen. Maybe if we are really nice, your mom will make us some eggs."

After Sam's mom left for the grocery store, he began to mow while Uncle Jason went to get a part for the bathroom faucet which had developed a steady leak. After Uncle Jason returned, he went in to fix the dripping handle. Sam pulled weeds from their small flower bed near the house. When they had completed those tasks, they joined forces to work on fixing the bannister on the porch that had fallen into disrepair. After making it secure again, they paused to admire their handiwork.

"Looks pretty good to me, Sam. What's your professional opinion?"

"To be honest, I'm not sure I really care at this point. I just want to be done with it."

Uncle Jason laughed. "Shall we go in and get something to drink?"

The two of them walked toward the kitchen. "You wouldn't happen to have some iced tea in the house?"

"I'm afraid not; we ran out a couple years ago."

"Okay then, what do you have to drink?"

"Well, there's water, and that's about it."

"Two waters down here, bartender."

"No bar jokes, Uncle Jason. It's kind of a sore subject for me."

Both of them collapsed into a seat in the living room. "So how's everything going?" Uncle Jason asked.

"How much time do you have?" Sam replied with a big sigh.

"As long as you need. After all, we have the rest of the day."

"I was going to text you last night, but I got too tired," Sam confessed. "I really need your advice.

Mom has this obnoxious boyfriend, and I want to find a way to make her see that he isn't the one for her."

"So what don't you like about him?" Uncle Jason questioned.

"Besides everything? Mom is so desperate to find a guy that she will take anybody that shows an interest in her. I'm afraid she would marry him if he asked, just so she wouldn't have to be alone. And to top things off, his son is the school bully."

Jason thought for a moment. "If you're really sure that this guy is bad news, then you need to talk to your mom about it as soon as you can. Pray about it beforehand, and let the Holy Spirit guide you. Make sure to be sensitive and not be too harsh. After all, the reason you want to do this is not to hurt her but to help her avoid heartache down the road. Does that make sense to you?" Sam nodded. After pausing for a minute, Uncle Jason changed the subject. "Any ideas on what you want to do this afternoon?"

"Uncle Jason, could you take me to get a basketball?"

"Why the sudden interest in basketball?"

"I guess you should know that I'm on junior varsity team."

"Did you go to a tryout?" Uncle Jason said with an incredulous look on his face.

"No, I kind of got drafted," Sam admitted.

"Tell you what, why don't we get that basketball and find an open court. I'll give you some pointers that may help a little bit."

"Thanks, Uncle Jason. I'll take any help I can get."

On the way to pick up the basketball at the local sporting goods store, Jason questioned Sam about his relationship with Josh. "So this bully that you talked about, did he ever do anything to you?"

"He ran into me at school when I wasn't paying attention. Other than that he has left me alone."

"Sam, why do you think he chose the tallest boy in the school to pick on?"

"I have no idea why he would have targeted me. Maybe because I'm also the skinniest boy in school." He then paused, deciding how much he should reveal. "What really concerns me is that he's threatening Valerie."

Uncle Jason raised his eyebrows. "So who's Valerie?"

"When Josh bashed into me, she stood up to him and got my books back. Now he wants revenge on her."

"Is Valerie your girlfriend?"

Sam turned red with embarrassment. "No, she is just a friend."

Uncle Jason smiled. "So let me get this straight. She's a friend that is a girl, not a girlfriend." As Sam struggled to come up with a response, Jason turned serious. "You know that you can report any bullying. Most schools have a no-tolerance policy."

"But other than running into me, he hasn't done anything yet. He'll deny threatening anyone if I report it. There's nothing I can do," Sam said helplessly.

"There is one more thing that can be done."

"What is that, Uncle Jason?"

"Pray for wisdom for yourself, protection for Valerie, and a changed heart for Josh."

"All right," Sam grudgingly conceded, "but I can't guarantee what I'm going to pray for in Josh's case. It might be a totally different type of prayer." They both laughed as they arrived at the sporting goods store.

An uncomfortable feeling settled over Sam as he entered the building. He couldn't remember ever being in a place like this. Did his dad ever take him here? Had he played any sport when he was little? Quite often, he would see a pee-wee soccer game taking place, every child running after the ball in a mass of bodies. There always seemed to be one child watching butterflies or picking dandelions. Was he that child? Sadness overtook him like a dark cloud blocking out the sun. Why did he have to be the one without a dad? Uncle Jason noticed his silence and the faraway look in his eyes.

"Sam, are you doing okay?"

"Why did my mom and dad split up?"

Uncle Jason motioned over to an unoccupied corner of the store. "That's really not for me to say. I was only able to hear your mom's side of things. I do know that usually, there is blame on both sides when a marriage doesn't work out. Both of your parents were stubborn and somewhat selfish when they married. Maybe they were just not mature enough to handle conflict."

"Was it because of me?" Sam asked, his voice cracking with emotion.

"No, Sam, not at all. It's never the child's fault. The issues they had in their marriage were strictly of their own making." Uncle Jason became more animated. With passion in his voice, he looked Sam straight in the eye. "Don't ever believe you were at fault. That is a lie from the pit of hell. Do you believe that?"

"I guess I do," said Sam hesitantly. "It's just that no one ever gave me a reason why they divorced. Mom refuses to talk about it, and I never see Dad. Sometimes, I feel like I must have been a really bad kid for Dad to take off and never come back to see me."

"Remember, Sam, that is his issue, not yours."

"I get what you're saying, but I just need to be reminded of that once in a while."

"If you forget what the truth is, come talk to your Uncle Jason, okay? Now, let's go pick out a good basketball."

After deciding on a basketball, the two of them searched for an unoccupied court. Sam was insistent that nobody be around to watch him. He felt really self-conscious about his awkwardness and lack of basketball skills. On a beautiful fall day like this one, it was hard to find an empty spot anywhere. Reluctantly, Sam suggested the elementary school near his house.

Uncle Jason pulled his car into a vacant space in the parking lot. There seemingly was not a soul around. The basketball hoops were in the back of the school, so you couldn't tell if someone was there unless you heard the sounds of kids playing. It was quiet when they went around the side of the school.

"Looks like we're in luck. The court is all ours, Sam. I haven't shot hoops for such a long time. It brings back memories of being young. C'mon, let's go play," he said with excitement.

Sam warily stepped out, searching the nearby playground for movement of any sort. Noticing Sam eyeing the slides and other equipment, Uncle Jason hollered out to him. "If you want to go down the slide we can do that later."

Sam felt his cheeks turn red as he turned back toward the basketball hoop. "Sorry, I guess I'm a little paranoid." As Uncle Jason fired up a jump shot from three-point range, Sam took one last glance for two young boys who might be watching.

Sam was actually finding himself enjoying shooting baskets. Just being with Uncle Jason made for a good day for him, but he also felt a sense of accomplishment when he made a basket or got a rebound before his uncle. After shooting around for about a half hour, Uncle Jason pulled Sam aside.

"Okay, I know I'm not an expert at basketball by any means, but I've made a few observations, and I also have a few tips that might help. First of all, we need to work on your shot. You are not squaring up to the basket when you shoot. Also, you need to have a smooth follow-through after you take a shot." Sam was staring at him like he was speaking a different language. "Don't worry, we'll go through proper technique on everything we're discussing. Also, when you get a rebound, you need to put it back up without dribbling when you're on offense. You have an advantage when the ball is above your head. Most of your opponents can't get up that high. But when you dribble, the little guys can reach in and steal it. Down there is where their advantage lies, so dribble only when necessary."

Sam raised his hand to get Uncle Jason's attention. "How long are you planning to be here?"

Uncle Jason broke out into a grin. "I guess I'm getting a little carried away. We can go over a few things briefly and then head back to your house. Does that sound like a fair deal?"

Sam nodded his head in relief. "Can we stop for ice cream on the way home?"

"We'll see," said Uncle Jason with a wink. "It depends on how well you behave. Maybe if you are extra good, I'll let you go down the slide a few times."

Sam took the basketball and threw it at the legs of a fleeing Uncle Jason who was laughing hysterically. Sam smiled. This must be what it's like to have a father.

Coming home to an empty house brought Sam back to reality. Mom was at work, hopefully not with Ken hanging around leering at her. How would he be able to bring up her relationship with Ken so they could have an honest discussion? When would he find an opportune time to do that? Maybe Uncle Jason was right. He needed to pray. He hadn't done much of that lately. As a matter of fact, he hadn't cracked open his Bible in a long time. Why had he drifted so far from God? He knew in his heart that God loved him, but part of him resented God because his life wasn't turning out the way he wanted. He had learned his theology well enough but felt as if he needed, more than anything else, to have a restoration of his relationship with the Father that would never leave him or forsake him. Getting down on his knees, he prayed for the first time in a very long while. Tears streamed down his face as he cried out to God to forgive him. Eventually, a sense of peace settled upon him as he knelt on the floor. Slowly he got up from the floor, brushed a thin layer of dust off his Bible, and began to read.

After reading for a while, exhaustion began to overtake Sam. It had been a good day, but all the physical exertion began to take its toll. His eyes started to glaze over. Setting his Bible on the nightstand, he changed into his pajamas and turned out the light. He hated to go to bed before his mom came home, but he just couldn't stay awake any longer. He was too tired to be concerned about what would happen in his dream world. It was not like he had any control over it. No one knew about his nightly excursions, mostly because they wouldn't believe it anyway. How could he explain it to anyone? Sam closed his eyes and drifted off to sleep.

Sam's bed felt extra hard. Trying in vain to get comfortable, he rolled onto his left side. Where had his pillow disappeared to? Reaching out to find it, his hand touched the mattress. Instantly, he realized that he wasn't in bed at all. Opening his eyes, he discovered himself on a surface that appeared to be some type of precious metal. Looking over to his right, he was startled by the sight of an impressive-looking structure that rose up out of the metallic-like substance. Rising from his makeshift bed, he was compelled to inspect this new discovery. Feeling the surface with his fingertips, he observed that, while it was constructed out of a metal that he was unfamiliar with, it was smooth and soft to the touch. He could see that it had two stories and was as long as a football field. Large pillars graced the front entrance, reminding Sam of ancient Rome. Marveling at the architecture, he was curious what purpose the building served.

While he was admiring the intricate design, he felt a hand touch his shoulder. It was Hatsuko standing alongside him. "Beautiful, isn't it?"

Sam nodded his head in agreement. He gave her a wide smile. "It's good to see you again."

Hatsuko smiled back. "I am honored that you enjoy my company. Are you curious about the purpose of this building?"

"I sure am," he answered back.

"Then I feel it might be a good idea to go inside and let you discover just where we are."

The entrance door was imposing in its own way, with thick mahogany doors. It gave Sam no clue as to what awaited him inside. He gasped as he saw what it contained. It was a huge library, bigger than anything he could have imagined. Sam stood awestruck.

"I told you there were books here in our world. Have you ever seen a library with a bigger selection?"

Sam looked at Hatsuko with amazement. "There must be millions of books here!"

Hatsuko nodded her head in agreement. "I want to continue to learn new things, so I come here on a regular basis," she said as Sam studied the well-stocked shelves.

"What types of books do you have here?" he asked.

"Anything you can imagine is here, with the exception of any with content not suitable for this fine library. The best authors reside here, and they produce new works constantly. As I have said before, everyone has a job here that fits their gifts and interests. Would you like to see more?"

"Sure," Sam said enthusiastically.

They walked the main aisle of the ground floor as Sam tried to take in the magnitude of this place.

"Over here is where the Bibles are," Hatsuko commented. There were multiple copies of every type of Bible imaginable in a very large area. "Every one of the Bibles in the library was approved by the King. Any Bible that did not contain the entire truth was eliminated."

Sam was puzzled by Hatsuko's comment. "You mean there are some Bibles that aren't correct?"

"Satan likes to produce a counterfeit version of anything God creates in order to deceive people. Here only truth remains. Shall we continue our tour?"

"I have a friend who would love this place," said Sam quietly.

"Hopefully your friend will experience this someday," said Hatsuko as she headed to a gleaming spiral staircase leading to the second floor.

"What's up there?" asked Sam.

"All novels written by our resident authors are available on these shelves."

"Can I look at one of these books?" Sam wondered as he studied the vast array of choices.

"Of course," Hatsuko answered.

Sam gingerly walked over to the shelf and timidly took one down at random. Opening it up, he looked at it in a confused manner. "What language is this?"

"It is in a universal language that all of us understand in this world. Only those who live here know how to speak it. Someday, you will learn it too," Hatsuko said with smile. Her smile was replaced with a serious expression. "Possibly very soon. Come, it is time to leave."

After going back down the stairs, they headed toward a back exit. Sam took one last look at the inside of the library as he was leaving. When he turned back to go out the door, it was no longer there. Darkness replaced the light, and the distant sound of music could be heard. He realized that he was back in his room. It was time to get up and get ready for church. He had returned to reality, such as it was.

Sam listened for any sound coming from his mom's room, but there was only silence. She obviously was still sleeping. Did she remember her promise? Sam decided that if she was still asleep when he was done showering, he would wake her up. The hot water soothed his still aching muscles. He stayed in for a long time, thinking about what he was going to say to his mom. She probably would not be happy with him, but it was a risk worth taking. After he was dried off and had dressed for church, he decided it was time for the inevitable. Opening the bathroom door, he strode briskly toward her room. As he was about to knock, Sam noticed that a light was visible underneath the door. Maybe Uncle Jason would have two passengers this morning after all.

Humming softly, Sam went downstairs to make some eggs for breakfast. Hearing his mom come down the stairs, he cracked open a couple more so she could have some too. His smile faded when he saw her dressed in a flannel shirt and blue jeans. "That's a strange way to dress for church, Mom."

"You were in bed when I came home, so I couldn't discuss my plans with you. I'm sorry you had to find out like this, but Ken and I are going to watch some motorcycle racing today."

"Really, Mom. When did you ever have an interest in any form of racing," Sam said angrily.

"So what happened to going to church with us? I guess your promises are only good if you don't get a better offer."

"Sam Walker, that is totally unfair! It was the only time that would work out for both Ken and me." Her tone softened. "I am sorry that I'm breaking my promise. I should have never said that

I was going for sure. To be honest, I said it so you would leave me alone."

"Okay, Mom, since we're being honest now, what in the world do you see in that guy?"

"He has a lot of good qualities," she said defensively. "He has a steady job, and he treats me well."

Sam laughed sarcastically. "He's also obnoxious, ill-mannered, and a slob. Plus, you two have absolutely nothing in common whatsoever. But you would still rather spend time with him than your brother and your son." Sam waited for his mom to defend Ken.

Tears welled up in her eyes. "Don't you think I know what he's like? I'm not as stupid as you evidently think I am. Look at me, Sam," she said, not trying to hold back the tears anymore. "I'm not exactly a prize catch either. Who's going to want an aging divorcee with nothing to offer?" She continued as her voice began to waver with emotion. "I don't want to end up alone," she sobbed in a near hysterical tone.

"Maybe you should have stayed with Dad then," Sam said coldly. She instantly jumped up from the table and ran up to her room. Sam wanted to say he was sorry, but he really wasn't. She needed to hear the truth. His thoughts were interrupted by the smell of burning eggs. Grabbing the pan off the stovetop, he doused it under water. So much for a nice talk over breakfast.

Uncle Jason's car horn sounded in the driveway. Sam came walking slowly out of the garage and got into his car.

"Your mom not coming with us today?"

Sam shook his head. "She has other plans for today that don't include going to church with us."

"Let me guess," said Uncle Jason. "I'll bet her plans involve a certain boyfriend of hers."

"Don't even call him that," Sam said with a frown. He looked out the window, staring at nothing. "I think I blew it this morning. Mom and I had a big fight over her choosing to go out with Ken instead of going to church. I gave her my opinion of him and our argument ended with her running up to her room. I handled things exactly the way I didn't want to."

"Don't be too hard on yourself," said Uncle Jason sympathetically. "All of us have been there at one time or another. Maybe on our way home, we should get her some flowers, and you can apologize for hurting her."

"I think I'd like that," said Sam. "I hope she will too."

After church, Uncle Jason dropped Sam off at his house. When Sam walked in the door, he saw his mom sitting on the couch with a magazine that she obviously wasn't reading.

"Mom, why are you home already?" She didn't respond or turn to look at him. "I brought these flowers to you to say that I'm sorry for the things I said. I want to ask your forgiveness for being cruel to you."

She turned toward him, glancing at the flowers in his hand. Her eyes were red, and she had a sad expression on her face. "Those are real pretty, Sam. You better grab a vase from the cupboard in the kitchen," she said quietly.

Sam returned with the vase of flowers, putting it on the coffee table near his mom. She patted the spot next to her on the couch and motioned for him to sit.

"I broke up with Ken this morning. Everything you said earlier was true. I had just been pretending that he was going to change into something he's never going to be. The only person you can change is yourself, right?" Pausing, she stared at the wall as if she were remembering something. "Your dad and I were both guilty of trying to fix each other's perceived faults. We decided it was more important to get our way than to stay together. Unfortunately, you paid the price for our foolishness. I'm the one who owes you an apology. Can you forgive me?" she said in a trembling voice.

"Maybe we should both forgive each other," Sam replied.

"Would you just give me a hug, Sammy?"

"I will if you don't call me Sammy again. You know I hate that name."

"Agreed," said his mom as she wrapped her arms around him. "This is much better than fighting," she said as the two of them sat contentedly next to each other. Relief flooded over Sam, realizing that even though they had differences, they still loved each other.

The rest of the afternoon, both of them hung out in the living room. They were both doing their own thing, but it just seemed right that they were in close proximity of each other. Family needed to stick together through good times and hard times. Other than Uncle Jason, Sam didn't have anyone else besides his dad. As far as he was concerned, Dad had given up his right to be considered family. Soon, it was time for supper, and Sam contemplated what to make given the limited amount of food in the house. An idea hit him about the same time as his mom.

"What do you think, Sam? Should we order a pizza?"

"My thoughts exactly."

"Shall we get the works this time?" she asked.

"No way! Those slimy mushrooms are disgusting."

"It wouldn't hurt you to eat a mushroom," she teased. Sam made a face. "Okay, you win. Shall we go half and half on the pizza?"

"Sweet," he said with enthusiasm. "Let's order. I'm starving."

Later, as they sat in the living room relaxing, Sam decided it was safe to address some things about Ken. "I never told you, but the first day we met, Ken threatened to rearrange my face if I messed up his relationship with you."

His mom looked him in surprise. "Why didn't you tell me that? It would have made me question his character or, at the very least, his judgment."

"I guess I didn't know if you would believe me. I figured you would think I was just trying to sabotage things to keep you from dating him."

His mom stared at him in disbelief. "Sam, don't ever think such a thing again. I want you to be able to come to me with any concerns you have. So is there anything else I should know about Ken?"

"Well, since you asked, his son Josh is the school bully. I've had a few run-ins with him."

His mom shook her head in frustration. "Is that everything you've been hiding from me?"

Sam thought for a minute. "I think so. There is one thing that I'm curious about, though. It's strange, but Ken and Josh seem to have a hatred for books and anyone who reads them."

She pondered that for a minute. Suddenly, it came to her. "I think I know the answer to that one. Ken had a bitter divorce from his wife. She is a head librarian at the main branch over on Oak Street. He said that she was always pushing him to do some reading. So who knows, maybe Ken and Josh resent books because it represents Ken's wife in their minds."

"I guess if either one of them is chasing me, I'll just duck into a library," Sam said. Both of them laughed; for the moment at least, their troubles forgotten.

Sam read his Bible for a bit, and then said a prayer for Ken. It was a huge relief to have Ken out of the picture, and it felt good not to be at odds with his mom. He went to bed relaxed, but he also wondered what the night would bring. Whatever happened, he was sure it wouldn't be boring. Replaying the day in his mind, he drifted off to sleep.

Sam found himself rolling from side to side in his bed. When he was on his left side, he felt chilled and pulled the blankets tight over him, but laying on his right side, he got too warm with the blankets on. His bed seemed uncomfortable, almost like there were stones under his body. The pillow was even worse. It felt as if he was resting his head on a log. The sound of frogs croaking caused him to stir even more. It began to dawn on him that things were not quite right in his bedroom. Was his window open? That could explain why one side was cooler than the other. But why would he be hearing the sound of frogs outside his window? Groggily, he forced open his eyes. What he saw shocked him.

His bed was actually a huge mound of leaves on top of a gravel path, and his pillow the base of a tree. As he got to his feet, he turned to the left side of the path. In spite of the fact that it wasn't raining, the terrain was typical of a tropical rain forest. Beautiful orchids intermingled with a vast array of trees and plants. A few feet from where he was resting grew a rubber tree, oozing the latex coveted on earth. Fast growing bamboo sprung up amidst the crowded forest floor. Water lilies with their massive leaves spreading out for many feet provided a haven for bugs and small creatures. In a nearby carnauba palm, Sam spotted a sloth hanging from a branch. Searching for the croaking noise that had awakened him, he was startled by movement in an area of thick undergrowth. Silently waiting for something to emerge from the gigantic plants, he jumped in surprise when a frog the size of a large dog hopped into view. In the air, butterflies the size of an eagle drifted back and forth effortlessly. Beautiful tropical birds serenaded him as he soaked in the serenity displayed before him. Everything that Sam observed resembled its earthly counterpart–only in a perfected version.

Sam was so intrigued by what he saw that he hadn't even looked at the other side of the path. Finally, he tore himself away from the view of the rain forest, expecting to see a similar sight to his right. He stood staring in amazement. Despite being separated by only the width of the path, the terrain was completely different. The landscape was covered in snow as far as the eye could see. Snow was something he was very familiar with, but the magnitude of it was overwhelming. How could such a climate exist in such a close proximity to one that was the polar opposite? It should be totally impossible, but that seemed to be the norm here.

Sam stood on the path wondering what to do next. As he waited for one of his friends to arrive, a snowball went whizzing by, only inches from his face. Instinctively, he ducked as he awaited another attack. When none came, he cautiously scanned the area for any sign of activity. Noticing an unusually large clump of white in the distance, Sam strained to see exactly what was out there. Suddenly, Juan leaped up from behind a makeshift fort and fired another snowball at him. This one hit his intended target as Sam was too slow to react. The snowball splattered across his chest. Without thinking, Sam picked up some snow with his bare hands and tossed one back at him. As it sailed at least ten feet over Juan's head, he heard him laugh.

"You'll have to do better than that, my friend."

Searching for cover, Sam spotted a boulder alongside the path. He ducked behind it, bumping into a crouching Chelsea. He let out a scream as Chelsea instantly clamped a hand over his mouth. "Surprise," she said with a wide grin.

"What are you doing hiding behind this rock? You scared me half to death," he admitted sheepishly.

"I was waiting for you to stop being an easy target by standing right out in the open."

"Hey, I'm sorry, but I don't normally materialize on a path separating a rain forest and arctic tundra."

Chelsea tried unsuccessfully to stifle a laugh. "How can I keep from being noticed if you make me laugh out loud?"

"Sorry," he said in a somber voice. "Please forgive my indiscretion. So what's our plan, Commander Chelsea? I believe we have the enemy outnumbered if I am not mistaken."

"Stop," said Chelsea playfully. "You're doing it again." Sam gave her his best sad puppy dog face. "If you think Juan is alone, you are mistaken."

"So who is out there besides him?"

"My best guess is a boy named Sven. He likes hanging out over here. It reminds him of his homeland. I do have a plan of attack that I formulated while you were busy being pelted with snowballs, Private Sam."

He saluted Chelsea. "Yes, commander, please inform me of your strategy."

"Okay, this is what we are going to do. I want you to run out toward the snow and draw their fire. While they bombard you with snowballs, I will sneak around the side and ambush Juan and any accomplices he may have with him. Then you can join me as they retreat. Any questions?"

"Why are we not dressed in heavy winter clothes, and why weren't my hands very cold when I picked up some snow?" Chelsea gave him her sternest stare. "No, commander, no questions."

A PERFECT WORLD

With their plan finalized, Sam and Chelsea put it into action. Sam rushed to the nearest snow pile, keeping as low to the ground as someone his height could do. Picking up some snow, he lobbed it up and over the protective wall Juan had ducked behind. Anticipating retaliation of some kind, he braced himself for return fire. After nothing happened, he fired more snowballs at his target. Still, there was no response. Growing bolder, he moved closer. Could Juan have vacated his fort to surprise him from another spot? Considering the possibilities, he advanced cautiously. Without warning, a barrage of snowballs came flying at him. Realizing too late that he had been set up by Juan, Sam covered his head and ran full speed toward the direction of the fort until he crashed through the pile of snow. He landed face first into a snow bank as Juan roared with laughter. A blond boy stood next to Juan, ready to fire the next round if needed. Neither boy saw Chelsea confiscating their supply of snowballs. Acting before they realized she was there, Chelsea let loose her own offensive against them. They tried to escape, but along with Sam's help, Chelsea continued the onslaught until Juan raised his arms in defeat.

"You win this time," he acknowledged. He offered a handshake to Chelsea while Sven did the same to Sam.

Just before her hand touched Juan's, Chelsea hollered out to Sam. "Watch out, it's a trick!"

In an effort to escape, Sven pushed Sam, but at the last second, Sam grabbed Sven, and they went down together. Juan turned to run, but Chelsea dove at his feet and tackled him. All four of them ended up in the snow, laughing at the sight of their friends lying next to them.

Juan and Sven headed off to find their next adventure, while Sam and Chelsea returned to the path. "That was a brilliant strategy, Sam. You distracted them beautifully by pretending you thought they had relocated."

"Thanks, Chelsea, but I have to admit, I really did think they had found a different spot."

"Either way, it was a successful operation, Private Sam. I think you deserve a higher rank after this battle. So what do say, shall we ride some giant frogs in the rain forest?"

"Why not," he answered.

At the edge of the forest, a snake slithered by, causing Sam to jump back.

"Don't worry," Chelsea said with a laugh. "It doesn't talk."

Suddenly, a loud buzzing sound filled the air. Sam covered his ears. What was going on? Everything seemed to spin out of control, and he found himself becoming dizzy. He laid down to avoid falling over and then closed his eyes to block out all the trees and plants that were swaying in a haphazard manner. The buzzing continued relentlessly. Finally, the dizziness went away, and Sam dared to open his eyes. His alarm clock was going off in his room. *How long had it been ringing*, he wondered? Turning it off, he slowly got up, memories of snowball fights and giant frogs still flooding his mind. This was getting weirder all the time. Nothing at school could be as exciting as his nighttime visits to another world. Reluctantly, he prepared himself for another mundane Monday.

Before leaving, Sam peeked at the sky. It was an overcast day, and it appeared that rain was imminent. Wondering whether he should take his bike, Sam decided to risk it rather than take the bus. As he got ready to leave, he remembered there was basketball practice tonight. Grumbling to himself, he entered his room, pulled out a pair of shorts and tennis shoes that Uncle Jason had bought him, and stuffed them in his backpack. Strapping it on his back, he started out for school in a steady drizzle. Glancing nervously at the dark clouds, he rode quickly, hoping to arrive before a downpour started. Fortunately, the rain held off for the most part, so he remained fairly dry. As he parked his bike in the rack, he breathed a sigh of relief. Maybe things were starting to turn around. Today might be a good day after all.

Grabbing his backpack off the bike, he entered the building and made his way to his locker. When he rounded the corner, he froze. Sauntering down the hall from the opposite direction was Josh and two of his buddies. Instantly weighing his options, Sam realized he really didn't have any, unless he wanted to turn around and run. He would have to walk past them, pretending to be oblivious to their presence. Taking deep breaths in an attempt to remain calm, Sam braced himself for a confrontation. Much to his surprise, Josh walked by without even glancing at him. One of the boys locked eyes with Sam, and then quickly looked away as they went past. Sam was puzzled by the exchange. Why did Josh ignore him, and what was going on with Josh's friend? Shrugging it off, Sam opened his locker and headed to class.

After enduring the first half of his day, Sam eagerly hurried to the cafeteria. Spotting his favorite seat open, he laid his claim to it by sitting down with his sack lunch. He knew he wouldn't have to save one for Valerie because no one else was going to come and take that spot next to him. Eagerly awaiting her arrival, he pretended to be engrossed in his phone. Taking it out jogged his memory, so he sent his mom a text about his after-school plans. While he was finishing his text, Valerie sat down beside him.

"Hey, Valerie," he said nonchalantly, "how's it going today?"

"Not bad," she replied as she prepared to eat. "Why don't we pray a minute, then we can talk."

As she bowed her head, Sam found the courage to do the same. Even though he still felt self-conscious, it excited him to be less afraid of what people thought. When he opened his eyes, he noticed Valerie had finished before him.

"So you don't seem to be too concerned about praying in public anymore," she observed.

Feigning indignation, Sam asked, "Were you watching me?"

"Absolutely," she said laughingly.

"I guess we're even now," he commented.

"I'm not sure about that," she replied, "but we'll call it even."

"So what books are you reading now?" Valerie asked.

"Only the Bible," he answered.

"Good for you," she said approvingly. "I admire your dedication."

"Don't give me too much credit. I haven't done real well lately," he admitted.

"I'm afraid you're not the only one who has struggled with that issue. It's easy to get wrapped up in everything else that's going on in our lives," she said in a somber tone. "You know what?" she asked as her face brightened. "You've inspired me to do better. Tonight is a good time for a new start."

"That's me," Sam said sarcastically. "My nickname is Mr. Inspiration."

Valerie gave him a disgusted look. "You need to learn how to take a compliment."

"I'm sorry," he said. "I know I can be too sarcastic sometimes."

"Apology accepted. But don't let it happen again. You don't want to see me when I get angry." They both laughed. "Do you have basketball practice tonight?" she asked, changing the subject.

"I'm afraid so. Are you doing anything tonight?"

"I'm going over to a girl's house to help her study for a Spanish test. She's been struggling to learn the language, and she asked me to help."

"Who is she?" Sam asked.

"Her name's Maggie. She seems real nice. Do you know her?" Sam shook his head. "I'd better be going," she said as she finished the last of her lunch.

"Me too," Sam said as he glanced at the time. "Lunch went too quickly," he commented as he got up.

"It always does," Valerie agreed. As she started to leave, she stopped and turned back to Sam. "I enjoyed our conversation today. You're a pretty good guy, Sam Walker. Don't ever forget it."

Sam smiled weakly, unable to think of how to respond. He waved as she walked toward her next class. Once again, he could feel his cheeks turn red as he dumped his trash in the garbage container by the door. Maybe someday he could learn how to take a compliment.

When the buzzer rang to signal the end of class, Sam went to his locker to get his clothes and shoes for basketball. Plodding along slowly, he made his way to the locker room to change. Many of his teammates were already there, teasing and joking with each other. Sam shied away from the group and found a quiet corner to change. Being in the locker room made him feel extremely uncomfortable among the noise and macho attitudes. Finally, most of the boys left laughing and pushing each other. When he knew he could stall no longer, he joined them out on the court. He awkwardly jogged out and picked up a basketball.

"Not too fond of them, are you?" It was Nate, the short boy who befriended him at the last practice. Before Sam could think of a response, Nate eased his mind. "Don't worry, neither am I."

Tossing up a wild shot, Sam wandered over to where Nate was standing. "I just don't like the way they act sometimes," he said quietly. "Some of them seem to think they're better than everyone else."

Nate nodded. After casually shooting baskets for a few minutes, the players eyed Mr. Randolph who was striding purposefully into the middle of the floor.

"Okay, everyone, bring it in!" he shouted. All the boys circled around him. "Time for a little conditioning work. I'm not going to take it easy on you like I did last week," he declared ominously. Sam rolled his eyes. He wondered again why he had let himself be talked into this.

Sam stood bent over with his hands on his knees, gasping for air. Sweat poured down his body as Mr. Randolph allowed the team to take a break. Finding Nate over by the sidelines, Sam walked over to him after gulping down some water. "Doesn't Mr. Randolph ever sweat?" Sam wondered.

A PERFECT WORLD

Nate thought for a moment. "No, I don't think he does," he said with a serious expression. "Pretty disgusting, isn't it?"

Before Sam's breathing returned to normal, Mr. Randolph came back to shout instructions. "I want the first and second string out on the court. We're going to have a little scrimmage."

Cheers went up from the players. Sam gave Nate a quizzical expression. "We're over here on the bench," he said.

"Good," said Sam, relieved that he didn't have to go out on the floor.

One other boy joined them on the bench. "Name's Max. Welcome to the benchwarmer's club. We've got the best seat in the house for every game."

After acknowledging Max, Sam turned to Nate. "So why did you join the basketball team?"

"Because my dad made me pick a sport to play. I chose basketball over soccer so I wouldn't have to run so much. I figured I would never play at my height, and I could just sit on the bench. I didn't expect to have to do so much conditioning to not play. Shows how brilliant I am, doesn't it?

What about you? Why did you sign up?"

"I guess because the coaches wanted me to," said Sam with a shrug. "Unfortunately, I'm tall."

Max had been listening to them talk when he piped up with his own reason for joining. "Want to know why I am on the team? This is the best spot to see all the babes in the stands, of course. All the girls love a guy in uniform."

"I don't think that applies to our basketball uniforms," Nate said skeptically.

"I think the uniform thing involves the Marines or something like that," Sam contributed.

"You guys will see," said Max. "Hopefully, I don't have to go out on the court at all. I can't search the stands if I'm in the game."

"I don't want to go out there either," admitted Sam. "I don't feel like embarrassing myself in front of the whole school."

"Well, that settles it," declared Nate. "The three of us stay on the bench for the entire season."

"Which side do you think is my best?" asked Max.

"Neither," answered Nate with a smile.

Max gave him his most menacing glare. "Funny, Nate."

They were interrupted by Mr. Randolph's voice. "Sam, get out here."

Panic came over Sam. Unsure of where he was supposed to go and what he was supposed to do, he looked over to Mr. Randolph for direction. "Go in for Steven."

Sam watched Steven head to the bench and then went over to the spot Steven had been standing. Sam ran up and down the court hoping no one would pass him the ball. When the boy he was guarding got the ball passed to him, Sam raised his hands high to prevent him from getting a good shot. However, the boy simply dribbled around him and scored.

"Come on, Sam. You need to move your feet."

Embarrassed, Sam ran back down the court. Suddenly, someone passed him the ball. Not knowing what to do, he finally threw it in the direction of one of his teammates. It rolled out of bounds, bringing the wrath of Mr. Randolph down on him.

"Sam, you need to know who you're throwing the ball to before you pass it."

Once again, his opponent received a pass from his teammate. Remembering to move his feet this time, he anticipated the player's move and blocked his path. His opponent fired up an off-balance shot. Sam jumped up to get the ball as it bounced off the rim. Grabbing the ball, he put it right back up like Uncle Jason had taught him. He excitedly watched as it went through the basket. Silence filled the gym, followed by nervous laughter. It was then he realized he had shot it into the wrong basket.

"Steven," yelled Mr. Randolph. "Go in for Sam."

"Hey, good job, dude," said Max. "You made it back here a lot sooner than I thought possible." Sam wanted to disappear. This was going from bad to worse.

A PERFECT WORLD

After briefly showering, Sam hurriedly got dressed, hoping no one would comment on his performance. Exiting the locker room, he peeked his head out to see if anyone was there. Wanting to avoid Mr. Randolph, he snuck out the first available exit, even though his bike was on the other side of the school. Letting out a sigh of relief, he jogged over to his bike. When he rounded the corner of the building, he saw a shadowy figure standing by his bike. Cautiously moving closer, he was able to make out the face of the person standing there. It was Josh's friend, the one who had locked eyes with him this morning. Obviously uncomfortable and soaking wet from the now steady rain, he approached Sam. Bracing himself for anything, Sam stopped a few feet away.

"What do you want?" he called out.

Josh's pal looked down at his feet. "I'm Gabe. I need to tell you something. Josh is getting his revenge on that red-haired girl tonight." Alarmed, Sam listened intently. "It ain't right. She don't deserve to be treated like that."

"What's he going to do?" Sam asked fearfully.

"He's got a girl named Maggie helping him. Josh is going to cut off most of Red's hair."

"Where does Maggie live?"

"I got her address here," Gabe said as he pulled out a damp piece of paper. "Just don't say nothin' about how you found out, promise?"

"Sure," said Sam as he worked feverishly to unhook his bike. "Thanks," he shouted as he rode off to find Maggie's house. Sam momentarily questioned if this could be some kind of setup, but concluded that he couldn't take the chance.

Sam was familiar with the street Maggie lived on; he just needed to find the house. The rain picked up in intensity, making it hard to see. He was swiftly coming up to her street; he only needed to figure out which direction to take. Adrenaline surged through his body, allowing him to pedal faster than his tired body should be able to go. There was no plan of action other than to get there as soon as possible. He came to the intersection of Maggie's street. Straining in vain to see addresses, he chose to go right. He finally was able to make out some numbers on the mailboxes. The realization that he was going the wrong way suddenly came to him. He made a quick U-turn in the street, failing to see the black SUV coming down the road. The driver slammed on the brakes, but it was too late. The impact sent Sam flying over the hood of the vehicle, landing with a sickening thud on the pavement. His rescue mission was over.

The fragment smell of lilacs drifted over to where Sam peacefully slept. He noticed the aroma before he even awoke. He smiled, reminiscing about the line of bushes in his grandma's yard that he had never actually seen. He had no memories of her for she had died when he was a baby. Somehow, he knew those were her favorite flower. He envisioned his mom as a happy young child, skipping through her yard, carefree as the squirrels that played in their huge old oak tree. Uncle Jason determinedly tried climbing to the next branch of the oak, even though it was out of his reach. Eventually, he quit trying and began to dig in the dirt, searching for unique bugs for his collection. Mom laughed and played with her beagle, Lucky. Mom had mentioned Lucky once or twice when she talked about her childhood. Lucky had died of old age before Sam was even born. Sam had heard stories of Grandpa Lou, a well-built man who labored on the family farm till the day he died. Sam could picture him coming in from the barn for supper and Mom running to meet him. He picked her up with his strong arms and twirled her around, both of them grinning happily. He saw another scene; this time, of his mom and dad on their wedding day. They were a beautiful couple, looking lovingly at each other as they said their vows. The two of them faded from view, replaced by Mom holding a baby girl. Sam had no clue who the baby was, but he noticed a sad expression on his mom's face. A gentle voice called Sam's name, waking him from his slumber.

"Wake up, Sam. It's time to go." Hatsuko stood above him, waiting for Sam to join her. Extending her hand, she helped him get off the ground.

He looked around in wonder. "I really did smell lilacs!" He had been sleeping underneath a lilac bush in full bloom.

"I would hope you smelled something," she said. "You had a very fragrant bed last night."

Sam studied the landscape surrounding them. They were in the middle of what had to be the largest garden ever. Rows and rows of plants went on as far as he could see. Some he recognized from books he had read, such as beans and carrots. Others were completely foreign to him.

"What is that with the square blue leaves?"

"Its name is beyond your understanding, but you will enjoy its taste." He bent down and pulled up a small vegetable that matched the leaves. Taking a cautious bite, he savored a flavor that was as sweet as his favorite candy bar and as refreshing as ice cream on a hot day.

"Do you like it?" she asked.

"Are there other vegetables that taste as great as that?" he asked eagerly.

"Many more, too numerous to count. However, we need to start on our journey," she replied.

"Where are we going?" he questioned.

"To the banquet feast in the capital city. There we will worship our King. Come, we can talk along the way."

Following Hatsuko's lead, Sam walked toward a large cornfield. The stalks were as large as small trees, so it was impossible to see what lay ahead. There was a small trail that began at the edge of the cornfield and appeared to lead to nowhere. Hatsuko confidently strode to the small opening.

"Are you positive this is the right path?" he questioned.

"You do not need to be concerned. I have traveled this road many times. I will never take an incorrect route."

They continued along, eventually coming to an open field. They stepped out of the corn and came to a pure, sparkling stream. It was fairly shallow, but it ran the length of the cornfield. "Let's get a drink and rest a moment before we wade across," Hatsuko suggested.

Sam was more than willing to take a break. After drinking from the refreshing water, they sat down under a tulip tree. "Are there others coming to this feast?" Sam asked.

"Oh yes. People from all over will come to the Great City. We will see many along the way, including Juan and Bakari. None of us would want to miss this occasion."

"Will I be allowed to come to the feast with you, Hatsuko?"

"That depends on you," she replied. "There will be a choice for you to make that will determine if you will enter the city. It is time to go," she said as she got to her feet.

Walking over to the edge of the stream, she took her shoes off and began to cross. Sam also removed his shoes and socks and stuck one foot timidly into the water, expecting it to feel ice cold. It was surprisingly warm to the touch even though it had been cool when they were drinking it. Sam smiled to himself. He was not fazed by anything he experienced anymore; he just accepted it. They both successfully crossed without incident. As they continued the trek to the Great City, they encountered a growing number of travelers all going the same direction. The excitement began to build as their destination drew closer. The landscape started to change. None of the plants or trees looked familiar anymore. Instead of a traditional green color, many shone like gold. Silver and other metallic minerals jutted out of the ground. A gigantic rainbow covered the sky, in spite of the fact no sun could be seen, and it hadn't rained at all. The majority of trees also had fruit hanging down so anyone that was hungry could grab a bite as they walked along. Everything was completely foreign to Sam, yet it seemed somehow familiar. He heard the sound of people running behind him. Turning to see what was happening, he saw Juan and Bakari racing toward them.

"Who wants to run all the way with us?" Juan blurted out in excitement.

Hatsuko and Sam looked at each other.

"Let me get this straight," Sam said. "I have two options, running as far as I can before collapsing or walking there calmly with Hatsuko?"

"Pretty much," Bakari agreed.

"So what's it going to be, Sam?" questioned Juan.

"Tough choice," said Sam, rubbing a beard that didn't exist. "As much as I would love to collapse and have trouble catching my breath, I think I'm going to stay here with Hatsuko."

"I am sensing some sarcasm again, my friend. Bakari and I are going to run ahead. If you change your mind, you can join us at any time." With that Juan and Bakari ran off and disappeared from view.

Sam shook his head. "Don't they ever get tired?"

"Not that I am aware of," answered Hatsuko.

"Are we getting close?" Sam wondered.

"Soon we will be able to see the walls of the city," Hatsuko answered. Sam could see the excitement on her face, anticipating the moment they would arrive. He wasn't sure what to feel. He sensed that his visits to this place were about to change for good.

Now the amount of people flocking to the city had increased substantially. They came from every direction, talking to each other, and seemingly enjoying the occasion. Every people group was represented, many in their native dress. Different ethnicities interacted with what could be considered their enemies on earth. Every person, though differing in age, appeared to be healthy and vibrant. Sam noticed there were no sick or injured among the crowd.

"Hatsuko, are there hospitals or doctors here?"

"No, of course not," she replied. "They are not needed because there is no sickness or disease."

"How can that be?" Sam wondered.

"All sickness and death have been eliminated by the King. No more suffering, and no more pain will be allowed ever again." Picking up the pace, she addressed Sam. "Let's hurry now. Right around this grove of trees, you will get your first glance of the city."

Eager to take a peek, he ran ahead. Searching for permission from Hatsuko, he turned and looked back at her just before he got to the tree line. She reassured him with a nod of approval. When he rounded the bend, he stopped and stared at the sight of a wall that rose up to block the view of the city.

The high wall that surrounded the city had multiple gates on the side facing him, leading to the assumption of more gates on the opposite side. The walls seemed to have been constructed out of a metal that glistened in the light. Each gate had an imposing figure standing by it. The figures were so large that even from a distance, Sam could see just how massive they were. Evidently, they were guarding each gate. Hatsuko caught up with Sam and stood alongside him as he scoured the scene with his eyes.

"What material is the wall made of?" he asked her.

"Jasper," she answered. "It is a type of stone found here. Shall we continue toward our destination?" As they walked closer, Hatsuko gave him more information about the walls. "When we get near, you will see that the foundations are made of different types of precious stones, varying in color and shape."

Noticing Sam straining to see the gates, she gave him a brief description. "There are twelve gates, each one created out of a single pearl."

Sam looked at her in amazement. "Who are those huge guards by each gate?"

"They are the King's most trusted servants."

Behind the walls, a glow came from the city. Sam's curiosity was driving him to move quickly to the gate. He longed to see what was inside.

He saw Juan and Bakari standing together by the entrance of one of the gates. Sam headed their direction without asking Hatsuko. They acknowledged him with goofy-looking handshakes that they had evidently created. Sam smiled at the sight of his friends' greeting.

"It's time for us to go in. Are you coming?" Juan asked.

"I really don't know," Sam replied.

"Either way, we will see each other again," Juan said with a wave of his hand. Juan and Bakari entered the city and disappeared into a sea of people.

As Sam watched them go, he felt a wave of sadness come over him. They had become good friends. He hoped he would be joining them soon.

Hatsuko put a hand on his shoulder. "Would you like to peek inside?"

Trembling with anticipation, Sam moved into the entryway. Everything he could see was made of pure gold. There was also a golden street running down the middle of the city, as transparent as glass. The street was divided by a river that ran down the middle of it. The water was as clear as crystal as it flowed down from a spot that rose above the rest of the street. Sam was unable, from his vantage point, to see what the source of the water was. He could see a tree that was split, half on each side of the river. There were different types of fruit on the tree, six on each side. Overwhelmed by everything he was seeing, Sam took a step back to where Hatsuko was standing.

She smiled compassionately at him. "I must go now. You need to remain here."

"Wait," said Sam with alarm, "how am I supposed to know what to do?"

"It will be explained to you. Please trust me. We will meet again." He watched her walk into the city until she was out of view.

———•———

Elizabeth Walker sat praying in the waiting room, nervously awaiting a report from the doctors. With tears flowing down her cheeks, she cried out to God. Her brother Jason paced, unable to sit in one spot. He too prayed as he walked in circles over and over again. He had immediately called the prayer line at church when he heard the news. Valerie also was in the room, attempting to encourage Elizabeth. The last report had not been encouraging as Sam was rushed into surgery to relieve bleeding on the brain. It had been hours since they had heard anything. Elizabeth was growing more and more distraught with each passing minute. Jason noticed her mental state deteriorating, so he stopped his pacing and sat in the empty chair alongside Elizabeth.

"I can't lose him, Jason. He's all I have left."

"Don't assume the worst, Elizabeth. We have a big God that can do miracles. The whole church is praying for him." Beginning to choke up himself, he turned away so she couldn't see his own tears sliding down his face. He needed to be strong for his sister's sake.

Valerie stepped in to cover for him. "Sam's going to make it, Mrs. Walker. He has lots of reasons to live." With a determined voice she declared, "He is not going to die!"

A door opened, and a weary looking doctor walked slowly over to Elizabeth. "We've done all we can at this time, Mrs. Walker. The next forty-eight hours will be critical. To be honest with you, quite often, it comes down to the patient's will to live. He's young and healthy enough to survive this accident, but he has to have the desire to fight as hard as he can. Give us a few minutes, and you can go in and see him," he said sympathetically. "Someone will come and get you soon."

Sam stood helplessly as people continued to enter the gates of the kingdom. He began to pace back and forth, making sure to avoid the large attendant of the gate. There were a few familiar faces, such as Masika and Sven. Others that he recognized joined the throng surging in.

"Sam," called out a female voice.

Searching the crowd, he spotted Chelsea waving her arms to get his attention. Relief flooded over him as he hurried over to her. "Am I glad to see you!"

"Sorry I'm late. Punctuality has never been my strong point," she said with a grin. "Why don't we go sit on the grass, and I will explain everything to you." They found a quiet spot under a redbud tree. "I know you have been wondering about this world." Sam nodded in agreement. "We are in Heaven," she said as she paused to let it sink in.

"But that's impossible," he scoffed. "I would have to be dead." Suddenly, his eyes got bigger. "I'm not dead, am I?"

"Technically, no," she answered. "You have been in a serious accident, however. There is a possibility that you soon will be."

"Wait," he said with a dazed expression. "Does that mean everyone here has died?"

"On earth, yes. But here, we live because of our Savior, Jesus Christ."

Still trying to comprehend everything, Sam attempted to sort out his thoughts. "So, what happened to Juan and Bakari?"

"Juan was killed by a drug cartel. Bakari was forced to flee his country because of civil war. He passed away from starvation."

"What about Hatsuko?"

"House fire. Others that you have met died of disease, shootings, or accidents."

"I thought there was no sorrow or tears in Heaven?" Sam wondered.

"How can I be sad about things that never were when I am living in a perfect world with the Creator and my Lord and Savior, Jesus Christ?" She paused to let her words sink in. "We are allowed to remember things that happened on earth only if God desires." He could see the love she had for him by the compassionate smile on her face. "Sometimes, He will reveal a memory through an angel."

He gave her an incredulous look. "An angel?"

She smiled at him. "Correct. Like the one guarding the gate that you've been trying to avoid."

Sam turned and cautiously glanced back at the gate. His face turned white. "I was standing right next to an angel!"

Chelsea roared with laughter. "Relax. They're the good guys, you know."

The color slowly returned to his face. Taking a deep breath to calm his nerves, Sam remembered that he hadn't asked Chelsea what had happened to her on earth. "So, what did you die of?" he asked in a somber voice.

"I was very ill as a baby. I only lived a few weeks. My mom, Elizabeth Walker, was especially devastated."

"That's a weird coincidence. My mom has the exact same name," Sam said with a puzzled expression.

"It's no coincidence," Chelsea gently replied, "because you're my brother."

Sam stood there stunned. Of all the surprises that Sam had received, this one was the biggest of all.

"How can that be? I don't understand."

"I was born the year before you. Because I never made it out of the hospital, there are no pictures of me at home. The ones taken at the hospital were hidden from view by Mom. She wasn't able to handle the emotional stress of telling you the truth."

Sam was beginning to comprehend the magnitude of all that was taking place. "Did that have anything to do with Mom and Dad's divorce?"

"Possibly. Dad never understood why she could never move on with her life better than she did. He told her that she was living in the past instead of the present."

"Wait, how could you know that if you were in Heaven already?" Sam asked.

"Did you forget about the angels? They are constantly ministering to the needs of those on the earth. Sometimes, they can be quite chatty about what they see," Chelsea said jokingly. Turning serious, she explained why she was permitted to have a glimpse into her parent's lives. "The reason God showed me these things is to help you make your decision."

"What do I need to decide?" he wondered out loud.

"If you want to stay here or go back home."

Sam stared at the city gates. All his friends were here except for Valerie. He wouldn't have to face bullies or do maintenance on a run-down house. There would be no more rotten boyfriends to tolerate or arguments with Mom. Here, there was no more sorrow and no more pain. The best part was yet to come, when he would be able to worship Jesus and go to the wedding feast. He did feel regret about leaving his mom and Uncle Jason. But was that enough reason to stay on earth, suffering in a sinful world?

"I have one more thing for you to see before you choose," Chelsea said. "Come over to the gates with me."

They walked up to the entrance. Standing just inside were a group of people. When they saw Sam, their faces lit up with excitement. Instantly, he knew that two of them were his grandparents. He recognized his Sunday school teacher, Mr. Otto, and one of mom's friends that had died of cancer. Scanning the faces, he also remembered his family physician, Doctor Stevens. His kindly next-door neighbor on the east side, Mr. Roberts, was there as well. All appeared healthy and strong. There were others he did not know, perhaps relatives of some sort. They all seemed to be waiting anxiously for him to enter and the celebration to begin.

He grasped his head with his hands, uncertain of what to do. Chelsea lovingly put her arm around him. He burst into tears, clinging to her with all his might.

"I wish we could have grown up together. We both missed out on so much," he said in a shaky voice. He started sobbing uncontrollably.

Chelsea gently stroked his head. "It's okay, the best is yet to come. The past no longer matters."

Sam nodded as he attempted, unsuccessfully, to control his emotions. "I'm so sorry," he said with embarrassment.

"If you don't stop crying, I'll have to ask an angel to throw you out of heaven on your ear. There are no tears allowed here, remember?" Chelsea gave him an understanding grin as he managed a weak smile. Getting up off the ground, she addressed Sam. "I'm going over by the gates of the city. If you want to join me, just walk over, and we'll go in together. If you don't, that's fine too. Either way, we will see each other again. If you decide to return to earth, simply find a comfortable spot to sleep. When you awaken, you will have returned to that world. Any questions?" He shook his head no. Chelsea laughed. "This is the first time I've seen you without a question." They embraced each other for a moment, and then Chelsea silently walked away.

Sam awoke to the sounds of machines buzzing and humming. Searching his surroundings, he spotted a figure in the shadows. He tried to identify who it was, but there seemed to be a fog enveloping the room. Finally, he regained the ability to focus his eyes. He could see his mom sleeping in a chair near the bed. Sam tried to call out her name, but nothing came out. His body hurt everywhere, especially when he moved. Willing himself to remain calm, he attempted once again to get his mom's attention. This time he managed to get a raspy sound out of his throat. Instantly, his mom jumped from her chair and rushed to his bedside.

"Sammy, you're awake! Oh, thank you, God!" she cried. She hugged him then let go when he groaned in pain. "Honey, is it okay if I let some visitors see you? They have been waiting all night. I won't let anyone stay long. The doctor suggested one person at a time for five minutes maximum when you wake up. Oh, Sammy," she said excitedly. "The doctors had said how amazed they were by how rapidly you were improving, but to see you awake is such a miracle! I think I have been talking way too much. I do that when I get wound up, you know." Pausing to catch her breath, she asked Sam sheepishly about visitors again.

"It's okay with me," he said, laboring with every word. "But please, don't call me Sammy." Grinning happily, she went out to the waiting area.

Sam closed his eyes to rest while she was gone. He was so very tired. Elizabeth hurried out of ICU and into the waiting area where everyone who stayed to see Sam was sleeping. When Elizabeth entered the room, Jason stirred and then opened his eyes. Seeing the huge smile on her face, he instantly realized that Sam had woken up. Moving silently so she wouldn't disturb anyone else, Elizabeth walked over to Jason and grabbed the vacant chair next to him.

"There's no logical reason he should be awake yet," she whispered to Jason. "The progress he has made is amazing the doctors. It's almost as if he decided that it was time to come back to us now."

Jason fought off the tears as he embraced Elizabeth. "Maybe that is exactly what happened."

The sound of someone entering the room caused Sam to jolt awake. He opened his eyes to an unfamiliar face staring down at him. "Who are you?" Sam asked in bewilderment.

The tall stranger cleared his throat nervously. "Your mom called me when you had your accident."

Sam was shocked. Not knowing what to say, Sam stammered, "I never knew you lived so close." An awkward silence settled over the room. Not ready to accept the man who had abandoned him, Sam searched for a way to end his visit. "Dad, thanks for coming, but I'm kind of tired. I'd like to see Uncle Jason for a couple of minutes. Can you send him in?"

His dad started to say something, but decided against it. He turned and walked out of the room. "Jason, Sam wants to talk to you."

Greg Walker slumped into his chair, staring at the floor. Elizabeth walked over and sat quietly next to him while Jason went in to talk to Sam.

"How you doing buddy?"

"I've had better days," he grimaced, struggling to find a comfortable position.

Jason studied Sam carefully. "How did it go with your dad?"

"Why did he come, Uncle Jason?" Jason shrugged.

"Your mom had to notify him."

"You're my dad now," Sam said defiantly.

"We'll talk about it later when you're feeling better. Are you up to one more visit? The doctors said family only, but after being here all night, I think she qualifies."

Sam nodded his head weakly, but when Jason left, he smiled to himself.

Valerie hurried in to see Sam. She looked more beautiful than ever.

"You still have your hair," he observed with relief.

Anger flashed across her face. "The car collided with you right outside of Maggie's house. Both Maggie and I ran out of the house to see what happened. I turned around for a second, and I saw Josh sneaking out of the house. If you hadn't been lying on the road, I would have chased him down."

The adrenaline rush from seeing the people he cared about most was starting to fade into extreme weariness.

"Let me tell you about something I read," he said weakly. "Can you find a passage on your phone?" Valerie pulled out her phone and prepared to find the desired scripture. "Philippians 1:22–25, if I remember correctly. Can you tell me what it says?"

As Valerie read, he suddenly commanded her to stop. "Now read the last two sentences of verse 22 through verse 24."

"'Yet what shall I choose? I do not know! I am torn between the two: I desire to depart and be with Christ, which is better by far; but it is more necessary for you that I remain in the body.'"

Sam closed his eyes from exhaustion. Valerie attempted to silently leave the room, but a sound behind her made her stop. "I guess my basketball career is over, isn't it?"

"Actually, I never did care much about basketball," Valerie declared.

A faint smile crossed his face. "Me either."

Author's Note

There were two main reasons for writing this novel. First, to tell an entertaining story about the struggles of everyday life that most of us can relate to. Second, to show that Heaven is not going to be a boring place to spend eternity but, rather, a perfected version of the earth, with the added bonus of being with our Lord and Savior Jesus Christ. I have attempted to stay as close to what Revelation 21 and 22 reveal as I was able, while imagining the endless possibilities of life in Heaven. At no time did I intend to offend anyone or misrepresent Heaven in any way. If we accept Christ as our personal Savior, we will one day have an opportunity to experience the glories of Heaven for ourselves and truly see what God has planned for us.

About the Author

Mike enjoys spending time with his family and being involved in his church. He has served in children's ministry for sixteen years and currently teaches a kindergarten class on Sunday. When Mike is not working at his job, which he has held for thirty-four years, he loves reading a good book. Mike resides in the suburbs of Grand Rapids, Michigan, with his wife of twenty-eight years. He has two children and a son-in-law. He began his writing career about three years ago, and this is his first published novel.

CPSIA information can be obtained
at www.ICGtesting.com
Printed in the USA
LVHW092154270619
622613LV00001B/56/P

9 781645 591139